Foreword by Jack Crossley, to whom Dan Billany dedicated the *Magic Door* in 1943 . . .

As a young boy I was thrilled to be the hero of Dan Billany's book. Now, very much later in life, I am delighted that his wonderful work is being republished and that I can acknowledge all that he did for me.

I was born in Carlton near Leeds, the son of a miner who died after a pit accident when I was three. My mother was remarkable and strong, but she had no money, two young children and then had a tough second marriage to a man who drank all his earnings and also had three of his own children to support.

My future prospects were not rosy. My lifeline and my great joy was school and reading. I couldn't get over what was available to me. I devoured whatever books I could find. And then Dan spotted me and nurtured what talent I had. He knew that English was my subject and allowed me to spend all my time on it. When I left school - at 14 in those days - my mother made sure I didn't go down the pit and equipped with Dan's teaching and care, I was able to join the Yorkshire Evening News in Leeds as a copy boy.

From Leeds I went to the Daily Dispatch in Manchester followed by a six month holiday relief stint at the Daily Mail's Manchester office. That stint lasted a couple of decades during which I became News Editor and then Assistant Editor of the Daily Mail in London, pioneering an investigative approach to news coverage. I became Home Editor on the Observer and then Editor of the Sunday Standard in Scotland for three years. I returned to Fleet Street and ran some award-winning investigations on the Daily Express followed by a ten years as Assistant Editor of the Times in charge of news coverage.

I have had a very rewarding half a century in newspapers. I am now retired - sort of - but still regularly provide news and investigation ideas to newspapers and magazines.

I have been immensely fortunate and I look back with great affection and gratitude to a gifted and creative man who singled me out from the slums and gave me such a wonderful opportunity.

THE
MAGIC DOOR

BY
DAN BILLANY

ILLUSTRATED BY
JOAN BILLANY

A LOST CHAPEL PUBLICATION
✳

This edition published in 2010
Lost Chapel Publications

First published in 1943
Thomas Nelson & Sons

Copyright ©
The Estate of Dan Billany

ISBN 978 0 9557117 2 5
Lost Chapel Publications
Stoney Stratton
Somerset BA4 6EA
Email: lostchapelbooks@fsmail.net
www.danbillany.com

Edited by Jodi Weston Brake
Printed and bound by CPI Antony Rowe,
Chippenham and Eastbourne, England

When Mr. Rocket looked round he saw an amazing sight
(see page 6)

DEDICATED TO THE BOYS OF STANDARD THREE

THE CAST OF THE MAGIC DOOR

REAL	FICTION
Mr Billany	Mr Rocket
Raymond Gay	Alan Hope
Master Charlton	Jimmy Corner
Jack Singleton	Edgar White
Kenneth Chapman	Arthur Black
Squeak Green	Squeak Morley
John Cane (owner of white rabbit)	Leslie Rodd
Master Darby	Billy Bartlett
Len Whur	John Berry
John Baxter	Alec Baker
Master Allinson	Cecil Carter
Leslie Love	Maurice Lane
Peter Johnson	Leonard Jackson
George Marriss	Jack Morris
Victor Chandler	Gordon Merrit
Douglas Gray	Edward Grey
Jack Crossley	Jack Crossley
Master Westoby	Harry Lowther
Master Hobden	Master Borden
Master Hirst	Stewart Needler
Norman Proctor	Fred Norman
Master Barker	Wilfred Charter
John Sole	John Martin
Master Weaver	Eric Taylor
Leslie Brackstone	Meredith Jones
Denis Robinson	Bobby McManus
Master ?	James Lock
Master Barrass	Peter Fairweather

Maurice Giles
Denis Yates
Master Rand

Denis Smith
Denis Glover
David Rogers

LIST OF ILLUSTRATIONS

CONTENTS

AUTHOR'S NOTE

The boys in this book are real, all but their names except Jack Crossley's are fictitious. All other characters are fictitious, or historical, or both.
DB

THE MAGIC DOOR

CHAPTER I
THE MAGIC DOOR

Perhaps they were the noisiest set of boys you ever saw; or perhaps not, but they got more opportunity. Finally, Mr. Rocket had what seemed a bright idea. It *was* a bright idea for him. He told them to write a diary each morning, as soon as they came into the school. "What's a diary?" they wanted to know, and Mr. Rocket said it was a book where you put all the things you did each day, so that when you grew up you would be able to see what you had done when you were young. Standard Three said they didn't want to know what they did when they were young when they grew up; so Mr Rocket said, "Never mind about that, you write a diary and do as you're told."

So that became the regular thing, and Standard Three were not quite so noisy for the first two minutes each day.

The particular day on which It All Began, they were doing their diaries. It was about two minutes past nine in the morning, and Mr. Rocket was finishing the register . . .

"Now let me see every boy writing his diary," said Mr. Rocket, dropping a red ink blot on the register as he looked up. "That means you Alan Hope," he added.

"Can't I finish drawing this trawler?" asked Alan Hope.

"No, you can't," said Mr. Rocket with much irritation, for he had just looked down and seen the blot.

"You've made me put a blot on the register, you young fool."

"How could I have made you put a blot on your register when I wasn't there an' maybe jogged your elbow, else kicked your desk, then maybe I could've made you make a blot on your register, but if I was sitting at my own desk all the time when you was making blots on your register, 'n' you made a blot on —"

"Shut up, boy," shouted Mr. Rocket. "Shut up and get on. And what do you think you're doing Corner?"

"Please, sir, I've dropped my pen."

"Well hurry and pick it up, then; and if I catch you whistling again, Edgar White, I'll wring your neck. Hands up the boys who've finished their diaries. I didn't say run out of your desks, I said hands up. How is it you haven't finished, Black?"

"I don't know, sir," said Black.

"No, neither do I. Well, we haven't time now. Put your books away, boys. That's right, Morley, push all your books out at the other side of your desk on the floor, so you'll have to pick them up again. Now there's no need to turn round to look at Morley, Leslie Rodd. You've seen him plenty of times before, and you'll see him again, no doubt. Put your eyes on me. On me; Lowther. Well, what do you want Bartlett?"

"Please, sir, will you mind this for me till playtime?"

"Yes, what is it?"

"I don't know," said Bartlett. "I found it near the playground, and thought it would do to make a catapult."

It was a piece of metal, very grimy and dirty, shaped like a letter Y.

"Catapult, indeed?" said Mr. Rocket, glaring. Then "H'm!" he said in some surprise, "it's very heavy, I wonder if it's made of lead?"

He scratched it with an old pen-nib, and the metal gleamed through the scratch with a bright green light.

"Well, that's queer," said Mr. Rocket, "I've never seen green metal before."

"Please, sir, there's some writing on the back," said Bartlett.

"Um, so there is; it's in a foreign language, though, so you wouldn't be able to read it."

"Please, sir, what language is it in?"

"Er—um—Chinese," said Mr. Rocket.

"Can you read Chinese, sir?" called out John Berry.

"Who asked you to shout out, John Berry?" asked Mr. Rocket sternly. "If you want to speak to me, have the goodness to put your hand up. I won't have this calling out. Yes, of course I can read Chinese. I can read any language."

"What does it say, sir?" asked Alec Baker, wriggling forward out of his desk.

"It says—er—it says—er—go back to your desk this minute, Alec Baker! I won't have boys rambling about all over the classroom."

"Is that what it says, sir?" asked Bartlett.

"No, no, of course not, stupid. That's just what I said to Alec Baker."

"Well, what does it say on the thing, sir?"

"I wish you boys wouldn't ask so many questions. Let me tell you, it's very hard to read Chinese," said Mr. Rocket.

"Oh," said Bartlett

"As a matter of fact, this is what it says: it says—er—um—it says 'Made in China' because it's a Chinese thing, you see."

"Oh," said the class, disappointed.

"And," continued Mr. Rocket, getting better at it, "it's part of a tea-service. It's what they stand the teapot on."

"Please, sir, they don't have teapots in China," said Carter.

"Oh yes they do, in some parts of China; and who asked you to shout anyway?" said Mr. Rocket indignantly.

"What's it made of, sir?" asked Maurice Lane.

Mr. Rocket thought quickly. "Hem. Hum. Well, it's a special green metal called—er—viridium, I think; Chinese teapots are always made of viridium, sometimes."

"How can they be always sometimes, sir?" asked Jackson in sheer cheek.

"Don't you call out, Jackson," said Mr. Rocket sternly.

"Please, sir, I think it's a door-knocker," said Bartlett.

"Don't be silly," said Mr. Rocket. "How can it be a door-knocker? Who ever saw a door-knocker like this?"

"Well, sir, these two little things at the top might hold up the arms, and then you bang with the bottom part."

"What a foolish door-knocker that would be," said Mr. Rocket, with a gentle smile. You mean—hold it up like that," he held up the little piece of metal, "and bang with it—so." He banged with it as he spoke, and then an amazing thing happened; as he moved the piece of metal twice forward, from the empty air came two tremendous knocks, just as if he had knocked on an iron door.

"Wow," said Bartlett, and dived like a porpoise under his desk.

Mr. Rocket had nerves of steel; this was shown by the cool way he faced the situation. Somehow the piece of metal jerked itself out of his hand and fell on the floor. At the same moment Mr. Rocket remembered a book he wanted for the next lesson, and hurried to the cupboard to get it. The book was right at the back of the cupboard, and Mr. Rocket almost had to crawl inside to reach it.

When Mr. Rocket looked round he saw an amazing sight. There, standing in the wall of the room and cutting through the middle of the blackboard, where Mr. Rocket had written out 'The Merry Haymakers' in his best blackboard handwriting for the inspectors to see, was a splendid door, made of shining green metal, with black metal scroll work on it, and a decorated archway round it, with precious stones flashing in the patterns of the decoration. Even Mr. Rocket—who, like all school teachers, was immensely rich—was surprised to see so many precious stones. And fastened to the centre of the door, like a door-knocker, was the piece of metal which Bartlett had found. How it got there Mr. Rocket could not imagine, since in his haste to get the book out of the cupboard he had certainly dropped the piece of metal on the floor. But there it was. And with a grinding, creaking, squeaking, metallic noise from its enormous hinges the great door was swinging open.

There was a clang, and the doorway yawned wide. Through the arch—it was a Norman arch, Mr. Rocket could tell that because he knew all about architecture— through the arch beyond which shone a strange attractive light, strode swiftly and silently the figure of a boy. But what a boy! He was certainly the most striking boy who had ever come into the classroom, not counting Edgar White in his Scout's uniform. His eyes were as blue as the sea and as bright as the stars, and his hair was like sunshine. From his shoulders rose two silver wings, which were so big they swept up level with his head and then down again almost to the floor. His heels were also winged—Mr. Rocket thought that was too much of a good thing—and he wore sandals of gold. "What is your will?" he cried.

Mr. Rocket could not think of anything to say; and after glancing doubtfully at his watch, he said: "Can you tell me the right time,"

"It's always the right time," said the boy.

"Er—um—yes," said Mr. Rocket, feeling a little bit puzzled. The answer *sounded* right, and yet somehow it didn't seem to get you much further. Mr. Rocket thought perhaps he had better tell the boys there was no danger now, so he said to them: "It's all right, boys, you can come up now." For the boys had all dived under their desks and were trying to pretend they never had dived underneath. After all, they were only boys, and boys can't help being frightened when anything strange happens. They haven't the calm courage of grown-ups like Mr. Rocket. It was silly of them to pretend they had not been afraid. After all, there is nothing to be ashamed of in a boy's being afraid. And Alan Hope was so rude as to pretend that Mr. Rocket was afraid and was trying to get into the cupboard out of the way—as if Mr. Rocket would do anything like that. And anyway the cupboard wasn't big enough.

"So it *was* a door-knocker after all," said Bartlett, when Mr. Rocket had finished telling Alan Hope what a rude boy he was, and explaining that he had gone to the cupboard to get a book.

"Of course it was a door-knocker," said the Winged Boy, "the most wonderful door-knocker on earth."

"But Mr. Rocket said it was a teapot stand," said Jack Morris. Jack Morris was the sort of boy who would never leave well alone. Mr. Rocket was wagging with his hand for him to shut up, but he *would* say it. Mr. Rocket thinks he said it on purpose.

"A WHAT?" asked the Boy.

"A Chinese teapot stand," shouted the class.

Mr. Rocket went red. Well, you would have gone red. "Well they *do* have teapot stands like that in China," he said.

"It's the first time I've heard of it," said the Boy.

"Then why does it say 'Made in China' on it?" asked Gordon Merrit.

"It doesn't," said the Boy. "It says, in Latin, 'None Knocketh in Vain.'"

Mr. Rocket was blushing like a red, red rose. The boys all looked at him. "Well," he said, "if it had been Chinese, it would have meant 'Made in China'. Besides I don't think it is Latin."

"Of course it's Latin," said the Boy scornfully. "What do you know about it?"

8

"A lot," said Mr. Rocket. "I know all about Latin. I learned it at college, so I ought to know. What do you know about it, anyhow?"

"Well, considering I spent four thousand years in Rome, I ought to know something about Latin," said the Boy.

"Liar," said Mr. Rocket, forgetting himself for a moment.

"Say something in Latin, if you know it," challenged the Boy.

Mr. Rocket looked doubtful for a second, and then, seeing that everyone was waiting for him to begin, said hurriedly:

"Bellum bellum bell'm, belli bello b'llo, b'lla b'la bla, blorum blis blis."

This was not a big success, since everybody started laughing, which was very rude and just showed their ignorance, as Mr. Rocket pointed out. Mr. Rocket was annoyed. "What are you doing in my classroom anyway?" he asked the Winged Boy. "You're not on the register; how dare you come barging into a classroom as if you owned it? I've a good mind to write to the Director of Education."

"I didn't barge into your classroom," said the Boy. "You knocked on my door, so naturally I opened it. Wouldn't you open your door if somebody knocked on it?"

"Well, you shouldn't open your door right in the middle of my blackboard," said Mr. Rocket. "I don't believe you have any right to have a door there at all.

What's the use of my writing 'The Merry Haymakers' on the board, when you come and open a door right in the middle of it?"

"It wasn't my fault," said the Boy. "I didn't want to spoil your blackboard, but I am bound to open my door every time anybody knocks. All other times it is closed, but when the holder of the Magic Knocker bangs on the door, I have to open it."

"And can we go through it?" asked Edward Grey.

"Certainly," said the Boy; "this way."

"Stay where you are," said Mr. Rocket; "the very idea! How dare you go wandering away through Magic Doorways during school time? I never heard of anything like it. You just stay where you are and get on with your work. What would I say if an inspector came in and found the classroom empty? It is out of the question. And, besides, where does the doorway lead?"

"Into the Past," said the Boy.

"Don't be silly," said Mr. Rocket.

The Winged Boy looked at him and sighed. "Gee, what a bonehead," he said. "I see I shall have to explain." And he spread his wings and flew round the classroom till he reached the cupboard, on which he sat.

"First I'd better explain who I am," said the Winged Boy, folding his wings down his back.

"Yes, you'd better," grumbled Mr. Rocket.

"I haven't really a name of my own. I've been called all sorts of names in my time."

"I bet you have," said Mr. Rocket. "I could think of one or two myself."

The Winged Boy made a face at him and continued. "My father is old Chronos."

"Who's Chronos?" asked Rogers.

"One of the Immortals. You call him Time nowadays. He's the one who turns the clocks and watches. He puts green leaves on the branches in April, but takes them off again in October. He's really a money lender and a dealer in second-hand clothes. In his shop he has more shelves than you've seen anywhere; and on those shelves, piled up, there is everything each of you will wear, or has worn, all piled up with your own name on the top. The piles of things are all pretty much alike; at the top there is golden hair and dark hair, glossy and curly, bright eyes and white teeth, children's laughter and tears, birthday cake, school lessons, visits to the seaside, comic papers, ice-cream; and further down the pile, you boys have work, and long trousers, and your first cigarette—if you haven't already had that—and marriage, and children of your own: it's the same for nearly all of you humans. And at the bottom of each pile there is silver hair instead of golden, and wrinkles instead of smooth skin, rheumatics instead of dancing limbs, and the last thing of all, the little ticket which says you've worn all the clothes which Time had for you, and returned them all. Time never gives anything—he's a business man, and he never lets you borrow anything till you've returned what you had before."

"I don't like Time," said Jack Crossley.

"Nobody likes him much," admitted the Winged Boy. "And what makes him most unpopular is the other work he has to do."

"What's that?" asked Mr. Rocket.

"He's the Doorkeeper of History. His job is to go along shutting the door after each minute and opening the door to the next one. If it wasn't for him, History would get all mixed up. As it used to before there were men. When there were only gods, there wasn't any past and there wasn't any future. If you broke your arm climbing over a wall, you could go back half an hour and climb over the wall again without breaking your arm this time."

"That would be great," said Lowther. "If I broke the jar with tadpoles in it, would I be able to go back to the time before I broke it and have all the tadpoles back again?"

"You could do it in the old days," said the Winged Boy. "But now Time has to shut away each minute as it passes, and lock the door, and that means that once a thing has happened, it's gone for good. Poor old Time is always busy nowadays, shutting the door on yesterday and opening it for tomorrow, and everyone hates him for all the happy days he shuts away in the past,"

"Doesn't it make him miserable?" asked Edgar White.

"It made him very miserable at first," said the Winged Boy. "Nobody would speak to him, because he

12

shut the door and locked the past away. So one day he remembered me, his only son, and gave me the task that I have had ever since."

"What's that?" asked Meredith Jones.

"To unlock the door into the Past!"

"I don't believe it," said Mr. Rocket, but nobody took any notice.

"And can you open the door any time you like?" asked Peter Fairweather.

"Oh, no. There are two conditions: first, I cannot open the door unless someone knocks with the Magic Knocker; and second, I can only open the door into a time when it has been open before—I mean, when somebody else has knocked with the Magic Knocker before."

"And is this really the door of time, the door which shuts away the past?" said Borden, touching the jewelled metal.

"The very same," said the Winged Boy.

"And can we go back any time we like?"

"No," answered the Boy. "If you go through, you must take your chance on what there is on the other side."

"Come on; let's go lads," said Stewart Needler.

"Well I'm not going," said Mr. Rocket. "You kids can please yourselves, but I have my register to finish."

The class scampered forward and lined up at the door. The Boy stopped them.

"Before you go," he said, "there is something I must tell you." He paused, to get their attention. It was

13

usually necessary with Standard Three, to pause to get their attention.

"There may be danger on the other side of the door. There may even be death. Some of you may go through the Magic Door and never come back. You may suffer hard-ships, you may perish far from your own century. You may die a thousand years before you were born. Whatever happens, if you wish to return to the present time, the last boy who passes through the Magic Door must tear off the knocker and carry it through in his hand. Then, should you be in danger, you have only to raise the knocker and knock on the empty air, and at once the door will appear and you can run through into the classroom again."

"Well, I'll go last, and I'll bring the knocker," cried Jack Crossley.

"Lowther, you'd better stay behind," said Mr. Rocket. "You have some arithmetic to finish from yesterday. And what did I tell you about a half-inch margin?"

"Oh, let me go, please," said Lowther. "I'll do my sums tomorrow."

"Oh, go on then," said Mr. Rocket. "I can't think why you would all want to go running away into history. I can't see anything specially attractive about history. What's the use of the good kind Education Committee giving you such enthralling sum books to work at, and such exquisitely comfortable desks, and such glorious classrooms, carefully designed to delight the hearts of the children? Ingratitude, that's what it is.

Go on, go on; and mind you're all back at ten minutes to four."

Here Mr. Rocket looked up and found he was talking to himself, since the boys had all rushed through the Magic Door; Jack Crossley had pulled the knocker off the door, the door had slammed to and vanished, and Mr. Rocket was sitting in an empty classroom, looking at the blackboard, on which was written, very neatly, the second verse of 'The Merry Haymakers.'

CHAPTER II
BEYOND THE DOORWAY

There was a grinding kind of crash, shattering and heavy, and the green metal door slammed behind the schoolboys, and vanished from their sight; and strangely enough, each boy, as he looked round on the world the other side, was gasping a little—for coming through the door gave them a curious feeling like going down very swiftly in a lift.

They were standing in a dark and tangled forest— a real forest, which made all the woods they had ever seen look like well kept gardens. For the first time they understood how it was possible for the Babes in the Wood to lose their way; for the first time they began to have sympathy with Hansel and Gretel.

Nothing could be seen but trees and bushes and tangled wild plants, whichever way they looked. Nettles, convolvuli, ivy, foxgloves, brambles, ragged bushes of every kind limited the view in every direction. They no longer knew where the Magic Door had stood by which they had entered this world. The forest was exactly the same all round them; there was no south, because the thick branches hid the sun, and so no north, east, or west. They had no way of finding a path to anywhere.

"Though that doesn't matter so much," thought Jack Crossley to himself; "not so much as you'd think, because after all we don't want to *go* anywhere."

The boys stood in rather frightened silence for a minute, and then Fred Norman spoke.

"I've lost my glasses," he said.

This suggested a terrible thought to Alan Hope.

"Don't you lose that door-knocker," he said to Jack Crossley. "Else we'll never go back again, 'n' we'll have to stay in History all our lives."

Jack Crossley carefully put the knocker in his pocket.

"Where are we, anyway?" asked Charter. No-one answered him. Now that they were actually in History, the boys were not sure whether they liked it. They crowded round Jack Crossley, determined to keep near the door-knocker.

"I think," said Squeak Morley, "that we ought to find out what part of history we are in. You never know, we might be in a bad bit of history, and something might happen to us. Besides, it's bad enough to go about not knowing *where* you are, so it must be worse still not to know *when* you are. I think we ought to find out."

"Well, how do you do that?" asked Charter lamely, looking at the silent and deserted wilderness around them.

"Yes, ask somebody," said Merrit sarcastically; "ask somebody! Who are you going to ask, anyway, that's what I want to know? Where are you gonna find anybody to ask, in this lot?" he waved at the trees.

"Maybe you think there's a policeman there you c'n ask, an' I don't think so."

"Well we can't stay here all day," said Leonard Jackson. "I vote we set off somewhere."

"Which way shall we go?" said Borden, Martin, Taylor, Merrit, Jones, and Smith all together.

"Follow me," said Hope; "I'll lead the way." And they set off through the wild forest. Nettles grew thickly in clumps, and stung their knees as they trampled through them. In order not to lose the precious door-knocker the boys linked hands as they walked, and formed a kind a of circle with Jack Crossley in the middle. Somewhere in the rear, Squeak Morley and Merrit could still be heard arguing about what part of history they were in and how they could find out.

"It ought to say it up somewhere," said Squeak, "on one of those trees or somewhere, it ought to say '1066' or whatever it is."

"Don't be nuts," said Merrit, "you might as well expect it to say '1942' on the tree outside the school gate."

"Well, it does," said Squeak Morley, "'cos I cut it in with my Scout knife."

"I reckon there ought to be *some* way to tell," said Edgar White.

"I know what I think it is," said Leslie Rodd. "I think it might be Ancient Britain."

"Were there any wild animals in Ancient Briton?" asked Peter Fairweather timidly. .

"Might be wolves an' things," said Bartlett carelessly. "But wolves, they're nothing. Nobody cares about wolves."

Hardly had he spoken when Hope, who was at the front of the party, saw what looked like the form of a large grey dog appear and disappear among the trees in the distance.

"What's that?" he gasped, and his heart seemed to turn over. He suddenly realised what a great difference there was between a wolf in the Zoo and a wolf roaming about in the open.

"What's what?" asked Dennis Glover. "I never saw anything."

"Like a big grey dog," said Hope, conquering, by a mighty effort of his will, the sick fear he felt inside him.

A shiver ran through the boys at his words, and no-one spoke. The resulting silence was broken by the howl of a wolf in the distance.

"Oh my goodness," said Norman faintly.

"Hurry," said Hope; "perhaps if we keep right on we shall get away from them."

All the boys broke into a run, and Smith, being a good runner, soon came to the front. Dennis Glover unluckily hurt his foot on a tree-stump, however, and could not run fast, so the others helped him along as best they could. Running in the forest was much more difficult than it sounds. The boys could never really see the ground on which they trod, so thickly was it covered by trailing plants, nettles, and brambles. They were knee deep, sometimes waist-deep, in plants, from which every now and then they broke into a little clearing. They had not been running long when from a clump of bushes in front of them leapt a young wolf. Its lips were writhed back in a snarl from its long teeth; it was a most unpleasant sight. They spun round and raced away in the other direction. The wolf was joined by many others, and, looking back, the boys saw scores of the ravenous beasts loping along after them, their tongues hanging out and their greedy eyes glaring.

"Quick," shouted Hope; "the knocker! Get the knocker out and let's go back."

Jack Crossley already had the knocker in his hand: he raised it to knock, but at that moment a wolf leapt on him, and he went crashing to the ground, while the knocker fell from sight amid a tangle of nettles and brambles.

There was no time for thinking; White had his Scout knife open in his hand, and he threw himself on the wolf which had attacked Jack Crossley. A few stabs and the animal lay dead, and Crossley staggered to his feet, his arm bitten and his face scratched, but still prepared to struggle for his life.

"We shall have to fight for it, lads," cried Alan Hope; "everybody get a stick or a knife."

Few of the boys had knives, but they seized sticks and branches from the trees, and quickly made a ring around Crossley, Berry, and Bartlett, who were down on their knees amongst the nettles, madly scratching for the knocker under the bramble bush. No sooner was the ring formed than the wolves were on them. Grey and Jackson with a few heavy strokes killed a gaunt timber-wolf, but Corner went down with two wolves on top of him, and was only saved from death by Hope and Merrit, who killed one of the animals, and so wounded the other that it dragged itself away to die in the forest. But the courage and strength of Hercules would have been of no avail against the wolves which poured in on the boys. Soon the ring of boys was broken, and they were swept beneath a grey sea of snarling, snapping, writhing wolves. One wolf caught Edward Grey by the shoulder, and another went for his throat. It seemed nothing could save him, when suddenly a gleaming sword shore through the flesh and bone of the wolf which held him and severed its head from its body.

When the boys who lay on the ground, bleeding and torn, struggled to their feet, they saw a very different sight from what they expected. A dozen wolves already lay dead around them. A few other wolves were scampering back into the forest, pursued by soldiers wearing bright breast-plates and helmets, and carrying short double edged swords.

"Romans," said Borden.

"I've found the knocker," said Crossley, holding it up.

"Thank goodness," said Hope. "Put it in your pocket, and don't drop it again, whatever you do."

"Well, boys," said a tall bronzed Roman, coming up to them, "you put up a good fight, but if we hadn't come along just at that moment I think your bones would have been here tomorrow morning."

"You saved our lives," said Hope. "What can we do to show our gratitude?"

"Oh don't worry about that," said the Roman, "we shall probably kill you tomorrow, anyway, so I wouldn't bother too much about feeling grateful, if I were you."

At this the boys looked at each other, and Merrit said: "We haven't done anything to you, so I don't see why you should want to kill us. You're as bad as the wolves."

"Worse," said Fred Norman.

"Of course, he's only joking," whispered Squeak Morley to Leonard Jackson hopefully.

"He doesn't look very jokey," answered Leonard.

"We kill all Britons," said the Roman.

"Well we're not Britons, so there," said Jack Morris.

"We're Angles and Saxons from across the sea, only we haven't come across yet, not for another two or three hundred years."

"Don't be daft Jack Morris," said John Berry. "We must have come, else how could we be here?"

"No, but we are descended from the Angles and Saxons," said Jack Morris; "and the Angles and Saxons didn't come till about three hundred years after the Romans, and the Britons ran away and lived in Wales."

"I don't know what you're talking about," said the Roman soldier; "three hundred years after the Romans, indeed. Such nonsense. Three hundred years after the Romans there won't be anybody left alive, probably. Without the Roman Empire to look after the rights of everybody, civilization would collapse, and mankind would become savages again."

James Lock had heard something like that before.

"Oh, you mean the British Empire," he said brightly.

"Nonsense. Rubbish," snorted the Roman. "British Empire, indeed. The British are a wretched tribe of savages—as if they could have an Empire. You must be Britons, or you would never talk such nonsense about the British Empire. You come along to our general."

He turned to the other Romans. "Come on, men," he shouted, "let's take these Britons to Cæsar."

"Cæsar!" said Lesley Rodd, pricking up his ears, while Jack Morris said; "I told you we aren't Britons. We're English—Angles."

The Romans took no more notice of what the boys were saying, but surrounded them and marched them through the forest towards their camp. It was a very weary march. Dennis Glover was limping along with his injured foot; Jack Crossley's arm hung limp in his sleeve; all the boys were bitten or scratched in some way. They thought the journey would never end, and wondered at the strength and endurance of the Roman soldiers, who marched as smartly under their heavy amour as if they had just set out. At last, however, they came to a clearing in the wood, and found themselves outside the Roman camp.

The camp was square, and as big as a large field. It was surrounded by a large wall of earth, three times as high as a man; and around the outside of the wall ran a deep dry ditch, which was the space from which the earth had been dug to make the wall.

"I thought you always put water in the moat round the camp?" said Merrit.

"Not always," answered a Roman soldier, "often we camp near a river, and then we can turn the water into our moat; but when there is no water near, we have to leave the ditch dry."

"Where's the drawbridge?" asked Borden, who wished to show off his knowledge of military matters.

"I don't know what you mean," answered the soldier; "we can't waste our time building bridges to every camp. Come on." And he pushed the boy sharply forward, since he had seen the tall figure of the captain approaching.

The boys marched along by one wall of the camp, and round the corner, while the Roman captain marched beside them, looking suspiciously at them and muttering about what happened to Roman soldiers who sold military secrets to British spies. At about this point a diversion was caused by Alan Hope, who hit one of the soldiers on the nose and made it bleed.

"You shouldn't have done that," said Denis Smith.

"Well, he pricked me with his sword," retorted Alan Hope.

The Roman soldier threw his head back, but his nose would not stop bleeding, for Hope had dealt him a mighty wallop. Finally another soldier put his cold iron shield on the back of the man with the bleeding nose, and that seemed to cure him.

When they got this matter settled, they found themselves at the entrance to the camp. The wall, with its ditch, had not been continued all the way round, and there was an opening, which was filled by a wooden gate guarded by many soldiers. When the guards saw the party approaching they drew open the gate, and the schoolboys passed inside, closely guarded by their captors.

"What have you got there?" laughed one of the guards.

"Some young Britons," answered the captain of the band which had rescued the boys.

"Ho ho!" said the other, "they will provide good target practice tomorrow for our arrows and spears."

"I've already told you we're not Britons," said Jack Morris, "we're Angles—English people."

"Shut up, you," said the soldier near him, and struck him on the head with the butt of his spear, so that he fell down unconscious.

None of the boys dared to say anything for fear they, too, should be knocked down; but they crowded round Jack Morris and picked him up, and in this way the schoolboys made their way into the camp of Cæsar. Denis Glover by now was hardly able to walk, since his injured foot had swollen, and was aching and throbbing inside his boot. Jack Crossley was nearly fainting with the pain of his arm, where the wolves had bitten him, and he was leaning heavily on John Berry. Lowther, Merrit, Grey, and Bobby McManus were carrying the limp form of Jack Morris. All the boys were dog-tired, and were very glad when the Roman captain cried, "Halt!"

They stood still in a trodden patch of land in one corner of the camp, awaiting the next command. The Roman captain left them, however, to report to Cæsar, and one by one the boys slipped down to the ground asleep. Hope said bitterly: "Can't anyone bring us a drink of water?" At this one of the Roman soldiers, who seemed to be sorry for them, went away and returned with a vessel of water, which those of the boys who were still awake drank eagerly, although it tasted of mud. They then splashed some water on Jack Morris, who stirred and groaned, and said: "My head aches." Hope was trying to look sharply round him for a way to escape, but he had hardly time to see the horses and cattle, stolen from the Britons, which stood tethered in the corner, before tiredness overcame him, and he fell fast asleep.

In a minute or two every boy but one was stretched on the ground, in the soundest sleep he had ever slept. Their first excursion through the Magic Door had brought them more excitement than they had had in all their lives before. In one day they had been attacked by wolves, rescued by Romans, and marched for thirteen miles. No wonder they were tired. And yet they were not all sound asleep. Edgar White was stretched out on a clump of nettles, and one of them was down his back. It stung him so much that he half woke, and saw dimly, through his eyelashes, a tall thin man with a hooked nose and a bald head, who came from a tent at the other side of the camp and inspected the sleeping boys as they lay on the ground.

"What do you say these are?" he asked the captain who stood by.

"British boys, O Cæsar. We found then fighting a pack of wolves, and brought them here."

"I've never seen Britons like this before," said Cæsar.

Jack Morris groaned and muttered in his sleep: "Angles—not Brit—not Brit—Angles."

"Look here Sempronius," said Cæsar, "you'd better take these boys under cover and —mm—wash them. Yes wash them—they need it."

It was true. The boys were so dirty it was not possible to tell one from another; they were all alike caked in mud and blood—wolves blood mainly—so that it was impossible to recognize them. They needed a wash. A few Roman soldiers dragged them roughly nearer the spring, and soaked them in cold water, and left them to dry. The washing woke all the boys up, and made Rogers sneeze, but they immediately fell asleep again, drenched and shivering. Night fell, and the band of schoolboys slept far more soundly beneath the stars of two thousand years ago than they had slept in their own beds at home.

CHAPTER III
CÆSAR

The boys were wakened next morning by the lowing of cattle and the neighing and prancing of horses which the soldiers were leading from this part of the camp. All the boys were stiff and sore; Morris nursed his head, Crossley his arm, Glover his foot.

"If this is history, I like geography," said Taylor firmly; "let's go back home."

"Yes, let's," cried everybody; even Hope and John Berry had had enough of this adventure. Crossley alone was a little reluctant to go back through the Magic Door.

"Can't we wait till we've seen Cæsar," he said. "After all, just think how we'd be able to swank when we get back. Everybody in the world has heard about Cæsar and read about him, but nobody has ever *seen* him, not even the cleverest man alive. When we go back, we'll be able to say we've actually seen him, and maybe even talked to him. It's worth a bit of trouble to see anybody as famous as Julius Cæsar."

31

None of the boys agreed however, Crossley and White were shouted down by the others, who now wanted nothing more than to get back home. "Get the knocker out," was the cry, and Crossley did so, rather against his will. At that moment a Roman soldier happened to walk past.

"What's that?" he cried, as soon as he saw the sunlight flash on the green metal; and before Crossley had time to make a movement, the soldier had snatched the knocker from his hand. "I'll show this to Cæsar," said the soldier, walking away with it, while the boys stared at him with open-mouthed dismay.

Jimmy Corner suddenly started crying. "I wanna go home," he said.

Hope buried his head in his hands. "That's done it now," he said. "Now we shall never go back home again, an' we shall have to live in history all our lives."

"Maybe not," said Leonard Jackson more cheerfully. "Maybe we shall be able to get the knocker away from that soldier. Anyway, it's no use being downhearted. We just have to keep smiling."

"Keep a stiff upper lip, my father says," put in another boy.

"What does that do?"

"I dunno. I reck'n it makes you feel cheerful."

"What, keepin' a stiff upper lip?" said Hope. "Well, p'rhaps we'd better try." So they all set to work stiffening their upper lips; Merrit wedged his with a piece of wood underneath, while Bobby McManus held his lip in place with string passed through his front teeth and over his nose. Whether or not it improved their spirits, it certainly passed the time, and it seemed but a few minutes before a Roman voice behind them said, "Here's your breakfast."

The breakfast was an immense steaming pot of what looked like very dirty porridge. The soldier called it 'Frumentum', while Maurice Lane, who had once worked on a farm, said it was Frummity. The boys didn't spend much time discussing what it was, however; they had something better to do with it. The soldier gave them a large pottery vessel, rather like a cup, but like red brick, and told them to start eating. They didn't have to be told twice. After a certain amount of squabbling about who was the first to drink first, they agreed to go in the same order as the register at school; so Baker came first, and was the only one to have a clean cup—since there was only one cup. There was some argument about Jack Crossley, who, having come into Standard Three later than the others, was last on the register instead of being with the other C's.

"Jack Crossley ought to come after Charter," said Morley, "'cos his name begins with a C."

"You're only saying that 'cos he's your friend," said Bobby McManus, who was starving. "He's last on the register, so he ought to come last." Eventually, however, they gave Jack his porridge after Charter, because he had a wounded arm.

Breakfast seemed to put new life into the boys. Instead of the despair that even the bravest of them felt earlier, they now felt new hope rising within them, and

33

even began to plot ways and means to get the knocker back from the man who had it, and escape again to their own century. All felt more cheerful, so that Merrit removed the stiffening from his upper lip, since he no longer needed it, Edgar White began to whistle, Smith made those blowing noises with his hands for which he was famous when Mr. Rocket was trying to teach them arithmetic, Bartlett sang 'The Lambeth Walk', and John Berry took out his cotton-bobbin catapult and hit the sentry in the eye with a match-stick. They had not been cheerful long, however, when a big grumpy-looking Roman came along and said: "Rise, British dogs, and march before Cæsar."

The boys rose obediently, though Morris was heard to mutter something about not being Britons, but Angles. He said this under his breath, however, stroking his head tenderly. Meanwhile John Berry shied a match at the grumpy Roman, and hit him behind the ear. Then they came before the greatest of all Roman generals, perhaps the greatest of all generals in the world—Julius Cæsar.

Cæsar was sitting on the back of a captured British chariot, cutting his toe-nails with a knife. His hair was decidedly thin on top—in fact, he was almost bald; but as if to make up for this his chin was bristly. He would have been quite tall, only he was shrinking with age; and yet he seemed wiry and tough, though his legs were scraggy. He was not at all like a great man. "Now my lads," he said, when the boys came before him, "what have you to say for yourselves?"

Nobody said anything, since they were all too interested watching him cut his toe-nails. He saw what they were looking at.

"Usually I file them," he said, "but I've lost my file. Look here, Sempronius, will you be cutting them for me whilst I talk to these lads? Don't cut my toes, that's all."

Sempronius ran forward and began cutting away, while Cæsar went on talking to the boys.

"And there are many more Britons in this beastly little island?" he asked.

"I don't know," said Hope, "it all depends on what part of history you're up to. Is this your second visit, or your first?"

"Well," said Cæsar, "I don't see what business it is of yours, but I don't mind saying it's my second. And furthermore," he said impressively, leaning forward and digging Alan Hope in the chest with his long scraggy finger—fancy being prodded by Julius Cæsar! —"if I don't conquer Briton this time, I'm not coming anymore. I can't waste my time like this. Mind you," he added, "the first time was only a flying visit. I was back in Gaul the same year. That's travelling for you."

"We could go to Gaul and back in an aeroplane between dinner-time and tea-time," said John Martin— which was a lie because he couldn't afford it.

"I don't believe you," said Cæsar calmly. "I've heard these funny stories before . . . Ow! Be careful, Sempronius, that's my toe. And what's an aeroplane, anyhow?"

"Oh, you wouldn't understand," said Charter.

"If you can understand it, then I can," said Cæsar; "but never mind about that. I want to know the answer to my question. Are there many more Britons on this miserable island?"

"I think there's a good lot more," said Carter; "but those in the north are only savages, and they don't know how to get together and fight. It's the Britons in the south you want to watch out for. But if this is your second visit, you needn't worry much—you win this time."

Cæsar looked at him with a puzzled expression. "Was your mother a fortune teller?" he asked.

"No; why?"

"Well how do you know whether I'm going to win this time or not, when I don't know myself?—and I'm sure I know a great deal more about it than you do."

"Oh no, you don't. We know exactly what's going to happen—Mr. Rocket told us. But you ought to keep your eyes open for Cassivellaunus."

"Oh, you know Cassivellaunus, do you?"

"Well, we haven't met him," said Hope, "but we know all about what he did—I mean what he's going to do."

"How do you know what he's going to do?" asked Cæsar.

"Well you see, he's done it," said White.

Cæsar was sitting on the back of a captured British chariot cutting his toe-nails with a knife.

"I don't know what you're talking about," said Cæsar, "and you're giving me a headache with your going-to-do's and your done-it's. Ow! Do be careful, Sempronius. Now let me tell you, lads, I've already had some trouble with this Cassi-whatever-he-calls-himself. He has a genius for organization."

"What's that?" asked Carter.

"Oh, you wouldn't understand," said Cæsar smartly; "but, anyway, you can take it from me, Cassi-what's-his-name has it. You know, so long as I had to deal with separate bands of Britons, I was all right; I just cut them to pieces."

"That," said John Martin severely, "is nothing to be proud of."

Cæsar looked annoyed, and he took it out on Sempronius. "*Will* you take more care!" he said, swearing at the unfortunate man in Latin. This seemed to improve his temper, and he turned again to the boys.

"Yes, I just *hewed* them to pieces, sliced them to ribbons," he said with a defiant glance at John Martin. "But now this Cassi has come along, and I don't seem to make any progress. You see, he gets all the tribes together against me, and it makes it very hard for me to conquer the island."

"Why don't you give it up and go home?" asked Stewart Needler, who thought it would be fun if he altered history by persuading Cæsar not to conquer Briton.

"He can't do that, he has to conquer Briton, because it's all in history," said Baker. "Mr. Rocket told us, so it must be true." For all the boys knew perfectly well that everything Mr. Rocket said was Gospel Truth.

"Anyway, don't worry," said Black to Cæsar, "Cassi will beat you once or twice, but you will win in the end."

"How do you know?" asked Cæsar.

"Mr. Rocket said so," said Black.

"Well, you may be right. But I don't mind telling you that I don't believe there is such a person as Mr. Rocket."

"There isn't—not yet," admitted Eric Taylor, "but there will be in two thousand years' time."

Cæsar sighed and scratched his head. "Good heavens, what on earth is he talking about?" He muttered to himself, and then said: "And here's another funny thing. Where did you get those clothes? I've never seen Britons dressed like that before, and I've seen plenty,"

"We're not Ancient Britons," said Jack Morris, putting his arm up in case anybody tried to hit him again. "I've told you before we're not Ancient Britons"

"I know perfectly well you're not ancient," said Cæsar; "if you were ancient you'd have whiskers and a bald head, like me—though I've still got a little hair left, may the gods be praised. I know perfectly . . . Ow! Steady on Sempronius!"

"It's you, O Cæsar, you *will* keep waggling your toes," said Sempronius.

38

"That's right, blame me. It's nothing to do with me if my toes waggle—you're cutting then, you ought to see they *don't* waggle. If you can't look after a few toes, what use will you be leading the Roman army? What was I saying?—you've made me forget. Oh, I know. I know perfectly well you're not ancient; you're only boys. But Britons you certainly are."

"But we're not, we're English—"

"Rubbish, bunkum, stuff and nonsense. Of course you're Britons. Why, one of my men told me you were talking about the British Empire—now, would anybody but a Briton talk so soft? You're British spies, that's what you are; boy spies, probably in the pay of Cassi-thingummy. You can't take me in with a . . . Ow! Wow! For the love of Jove! Sempronius, will you be careful? You're cutting the toe-nails of Julius Cæsar, not slaughtering an ox. Don't tell me I'm waggling; I'm not waggling."

"Look here, Cæsar," put in Jack Morris firmly, "we're not Britons. We're English, and we come from the Angles and Saxons, and they didn't come to Britain till about four hundred years after the Romans. You see, you're going to conquer Britain, and then Roman towns will be built all over Britain—at Chester and Doncaster and Colchester and Tadcaster and York and places like that—and after about four hundred years the Roman Empire will begin to collapse and die, and the Romans will leave Britain, and then the Angles and the Saxons and the Jutes, the pirates from across the sea, will come to the island, and they will be our great-

great-great-great-great-great-great-great-great-great grandfathers."

"Phew!" said Cæsar, looking at Jack with amazement. "Could you say all that again?"

"No," said Jack definitely, "it took me all my time to say it once."

"You'd make a wonderful fortune-teller," said Cæsar. "Who's been telling you all this stuff?"

"Mr. Rocket," said Maurice Lane.

"Who is this Mr. Rocket?" asked Cæsar. "Is he a wise man or something?"

"Well, I don't think he's a wise man; he *might* be something," said John Berry doubtfully. "No, I wouldn't call him a wise man, but he knows a bit."

"He can tell ghost stories," said Rogers.

"Well Mr. Rocket or no Mr. Rocket," said Cæsar, "you're all British spies, and you'll all be shot to death with arrows before tonight, or else cut to pieces . . . Ow! I didn't say cut me to pieces, Sempronius."

"That's the last one, O Cæsar."

"What, the last toe-nail? Or the last toe? I say, what's that you've got my lad?" added Cæsar, turning to John Berry.

"A kind of catapult, O Cæsar," said John Berry. "You see, all you need is a cotton-bobbin, a piece of rubber cut out of old bike-tyre—the inner tube part—and some matches, and you stretch the rubber across like this, and then you put a match-stick down the hole like this, and you pull it back like this, and then you let it go like this,—see?"

"Ow!" said Cæsar, as the match hit him on the end of the nose. "Yes, that's a very fine idea. I might even be able to use it—on a larger scale, of course—as a weapon for attacking forts and strongholds." He turned to Sempronius. "Come here, Sempronius. Now stand still."

Sempronius stood still before Cæsar.

"Now see if you can hit him on the nose," said Cæsar to John Berry.

John Berry took aim and scored a bull's eye.

"Ow!" said Sempronius.

Cæsar laughed heartily and clapped his hands.

"You ought to have one," said Berry to Cæsar, "you could have lots of fun with it."

"Yes," said Cæsar thoughtfully; "only there's just one thing—we haven't any matches."

"Oh, no," said John Berry, "I never thought of that."

"And then, there's another thing," said Cæsar; "you see we haven't any rubber."

"Of course not," said John Berry.

"And then," said Cæsar, "come to think of it—we haven't any cotton-bobbins."

"No," said John Berry sadly; "it's a pity you Romans are so ignorant. But never mind," he said, as Cæsar did not look very pleased by this last remark, "I'll give you this catapult. You'll have no end of fun, flipping matches at Brutus and Cassius. I'll give you my stock of matches, too."

"So you know Brutus and Cassius?" asked Cæsar in surprise.

"Well, we don't know them to speak to," said Carter, "but we know about them."

"Brutus and Cassius are going to kill you," said Bobby McManus.

"In the Temple of Jupiter," added Edward Grey.

"No, it was the Temple of Apollo," said Leonard Jackson.

"When you've stopped arguing about where I'm to be killed," said Cæsar, "I should be glad to know who's been telling you all this."

"Mr. Rocket," said Bobby McManus.

Cæsar exploded with rage. "Confound this Mr. Rocket," he said, "filling your heads with such confounded nonsense. What does Mr. Rocket know about Brutus, I'd like to know? Let me tell you, Brutus is one of the nicest chaps I ever met; wouldn't hurt a fly, Brutus wouldn't. Why, I've known him since he was no older than you boys. He's my adopted son, is Brutus; you didn't know that, did you? I'm not going to have this Mr. Rocket going round spreading these stories about my friends. Just let me get hold of Mr. Rocket, that's all. Where is he, anyway? Where does he live?"

"Well, he's rather a long way from here," said Black.

"In fact, he hasn't been born yet," said Needler, "not for two thousand years."

Cæsar stared at them in amazement; then suddenly he began to laugh.

"I see," he said. "They're all half-wits, all lunatics. You know Sempronius," he went on, "when the Britons find a lunatic, they think he is holy, and they worship him. Well, this must be a band of lunatic children. No wonder they say such queer things; they're all plumb coco, loco, potty; right off their onions; nutty, in fact; dotty. Take them away. Brutus and Cassius, indeed; mind you, Cassius I don't trust. He's a bit shifty is Cassius, I admit. But Brutus—how absurd. Take them away and guard them closely; if these are the sacred lunatic children of the British, they are very valuable hostages. When we go out to fight Cassi, we must take the boys with us, and if the Britons seem to be winning, we can kill all the boys, and the enemy will lose heart and run away."

As the guards marched the boys away, Jack Crossley saw the soldier who had stolen the Magic Knocker. He had polished it, and the bright metal shone with an emerald light, and he had fastened it round his neck with a chain so it hung down, half hidden by his breast-plate.

The boys now had to wait several weary hours, closely guarded; at length they heard the sound of a bugle in another part of the camp. There was a tramp of feet, and soon they realized that the Roman army was leaving the camp and making its way back through the woods. Though they did not know it, the reason was that Cæsar had heard from his scouts that

Cassivellaunus had called the tribes together in a clearing not far away. Determined to crush the British chieftain completely, Cæsar had immediately ordered all his troops to prepare for battle. The boys were forced to march behind the army, with a further band of soldiers behind them to make sure they had no chance of escape. However, this did not prevent the boys from whispering among themselves, and they had not marched two miles before they had decided on a plan to snatch the knocker from the man who wore it, and escape. Gordon Merrit, who was nearest to the soldier with the knocker, was selected for the dangerous work of snatching the knocker. The others were to help him by throwing themselves on the man's arms and legs, and overcoming him by their numbers. They hoped that the sight of the Magic Door would so frighten the Romans that they would fall to their knees, or do something equally silly, which would give the boys the chance to run through the door into safety. All this plan was prepared, and Merrit was waiting for the signal from Alan Hope to jump on the soldier, when an arrow swished past John Martin's head, from a tree above them, and struck one of the Romans through the ankle, pinning his foot to the ground. The boys heard the hard crunch of the man's bones as the arrow-head went through them, and the blood oozed round the hard-wood shaft. In a second the Romans had scattered to the nearest cover, the bowmen had their arrows to their strings, and the swordsmen stood blade in hand. All waited tensely for the signal from their leader, or the sight of an enemy—all except the wounded man, who dragged the arrow out of the ground and tried to pull it from his ankle, he fainted with pain as he did so; another arrow passed through his eye as he lay on the ground, and killed him.

The boys wasted no time; as soon as their guards ran for cover, they were off into the forest, and had run half a mile before Hope remembered that their only chance of returning to their own time was with the Romans, since the knocker still hung round the neck of one of the Roman soldiers.

"Stop, lads," Hope shouted.

"What's the matter?" asked Lowther.

"It's no use running away. We've got to go back. That Roman's got the knocker, and if we lose that . . ." He did not need to finish the sentence, for every boy knew what he meant.

They panted back to the place where the ambush had occurred, but missed their way as they came near, and came out in a clear space among the trees. Here a terrible sight met them. An army of Britons was charging down from the hill upon the Romans, who stood waiting for them, sword in hand. Behind the swordsmen stood the archers, steadily putting arrow after arrow to their bows, and sending volley after volley over the heads of their comrades into the ranks of the charging Britons. The Romans never said a word, even to encourage each other in their grim combat. Their mouths tightly closed, they worked steadily with their bows, or sternly awaited the enemy.

The Britons, on the other hand, were shouting fearful war-cries and waving above their heads hammers made out of large stone fastened to the end of a stick. Other Britons had spears and arrows, others rode horses; not all of them had shields, and in any case the heavy Roman arrows often crashed through both shield and man. The horsemen guided their horses with their knees, and wielded their weapons with both hands. The war-chariots of the Britons were also there, with their long wicked looking scythes sticking out at each end of the axle-shaft. There was no discipline in the mad British charge; each man fought as he wished, but they did not seem to get much in each other's way. Even as the boys watched them the Britons swept on the Romans like a wave breaking on a rock. Amidst the savage cries came more horrible sounds: the sounds of hammers breaking through bone, the screams of dying horses, and the jolting of chariot wheels over men. Like ploughs the British chariots tore through the ranks of their enemies, leaving a furrow bounded on either side by a line of dead and wounded. But the Britons did not have it all their own way; the stubborn squares of the Roman soldiers never yielded an inch, but every time the Britons turned back they advanced a little over the blood-soaked ground.

As the fight went on, the appearance of the fighters became ever more frightful. The Britons, with their wild hair streaming, their faces and bodies painted with the blue 'woad' which was their war-paint, looked like fiends from a nightmare as they added the dark red of blood to their colours, and brandished their hammers shining wet with the blood and brains of their enemies. The Romans looked like grim and determined butchers, who would not rest from their work till all the killing was done. For a long time the result of the battle was doubtful, but towards evening the Britons received strong reinforcements, and hundreds of them drew themselves once again on the wearied Romans.

Then at last Cæsar saw that today at any rate it was wise to take what remained of his army back to camp, rather than stay to have them massacred. He sounded the signal for retreat, but at that moment the Britons charged again, and for once the orderly Roman army became a mob of men running for their lives. Amid the confusion the boys saw the soldier who wore the Magic Knocker plunge into the forest and vanish. They raced away in that direction but could not find him, and were looking dismally about them when suddenly Baker caught a glimpse of his armour through the trees. They followed him silently, and soon came up with him.

"Give us our knocker," cried Borden.

The soldier had his sword in his hand, and was in an evil mood; he leapt upon them, with his sword raised, but Smith stooping low almost to the ground, threw himself at the Roman's knees, and he fell. The boys jumped on him, but were not prepared for his strength. Though his sword had fallen from his hand, he fought them without it, and rose to his feet, shaking them from him as a dog shakes itself after a swim.

Then he turned rapidly, picked up his sword, and was about to plunge it into Peter Fairweather, when an arrow buried itself to the feathers in his back, between his shoulder blades, and its point stuck out a foot from his chest. He fell like a log, and Crossley quickly turned him over and snatched the knocker from his throat, breaking the chain. But there was no chance of using the knocker, for Crossley now found himself almost alone. Scores of Britons were racing down towards him, and the other boys were already scattering among the trees. The nearest Briton was only a yard from Jack Crossley, and arrows were whistling all round. Crossley followed the other boys, and they all ran for their lives.

In their hast they were partially separated, but managed to assemble again under an oak tree half a mile away. Here all was quiet, except that in the distance the sounds of pursuit could faintly be heard, and ever and again came a faint and horrid scream, muffled in the depths of the forest, as some Romans were overtaken and slaughtered. The boys rested here for a moment, waiting for Crossley, who came running up last. The knocker was in his hand, and he was about to knock with it, when Leonard Jackson made a startling discovery.

An arrow buried itself to the feathers in his back

"I say, boys," he said, "there were thirty of us when we came through the door. I've just counted us now, and there's only twenty-nine."

"Who's missing?" asked Taylor. "Call the register," suggested Jones.

"One," shouted Baker.

"Two," shouted Bartlett.

Merit did not answer his number.

"Where's Merrit?" cried everybody. They scattered and searched the glade for him, and even took the risk of shouting his name, but he did not appear.

CHAPTER IV
TO THE RESCUE!

Where was Gordon Merrit?

This was the question each boy anxiously asked himself as they retraced their steps to the last place where they had seen the missing boy. He had been with them when Crossley had torn the knocker from the throat of the dead Roman soldier, and therefore they decided to go back there and look for him. Well they knew the danger, but they could not think of returning to their own world without Merrit.

There in the glade, when they reached it lay the dead body of the Roman, now stripped of his armour by the Britons. He lay cold and still where he fell, but of Merrit there was no sign. The boys searched more carefully among the trees, but they found not a trace.

By now the boys began to be seriously worried; what could have happened to him? They held a short council of war to discuss what was to be done, and finally determined to find the main body of the British warriors, to see if Merrit had been taken prisoner; but they did not wish to get captured or killed themselves, so they had to do their scouting with the utmost caution. Silently they threaded the wood in single file, Hope at the front, followed by Bartlett; then came Black, Carter, Crossley, Jones, Rogers, Martin, Lowther, Baker, Taylor, Borden, McManus, Morley, Rodd, Lane, Smith, Fairweather, Needler, Grey, Jackson, Glover, Berry, Morris, Charter, White, Norman, Lock, and Corner. At length, after a search that seemed to last for hours, they came up with the rearguard of the Britons, who were returning through the woods to a village where they had met for battle, and where they intended to feast to celebrate their victory. They had no prisoners, since their practice was to kill all enemies who fell into their hands; but just as the boys were turning away in despair, they saw a small party of Britons carrying on their shoulders a stout pole, to which the missing boy was tied by many ropes. The schoolboys now followed the Britons like twenty-nine shadows, darting silently through the trees and waiting for a chance to rescue Merrit; but no such chance occurred. However, by following close they were able to find out what the Britons meant to do with the boy. Just as the Romans—knowing clearly that the boys were not Roman, from their strange dress—had been sure they were Britons, so the Britons, knowing that no British boys were dressed like that, decided they must be Roman boys; and when they captured Merrit, they determined to burn him alive as a sacrifice to their gods in honour of the victory which they had won. Though he knew of the fate which was in store for him, Gordon Merrit was by no means downhearted, for his eyes, sharper than those of his captors, picked out the shadowy figures of the other boys stealing through the woods beside the victorious Britons, and he even caught the gleam of Hope's ginger hair behind a clump of brambles. A little later, Glover popped his head up and winked, and Merrit winked back.

When the Britons came into the village, the boys had their first sight of the Ancient British houses. These were tiny low huts made of trees and mud, sometimes with big stones built into the walls: and at one end of the village there were a few caves in a steep hillside, which were also used as houses. Around the village, as protection against enemies, ran a close high fence of stakes driven into the ground; and it was by peeping through the stakes which composed the fence that the boys now had to follow the adventures of their captured friend; for the army had passed through the gate, and of course the boys dared not show themselves there. The first thing the Britons did when they came into the village was to get drunk on a kind of drink they called mead; and whilst they were drunk, some of them quarreled about the spoils which they had won in battle, and one man was killed in a little argument that arose. As night drew on, however, the Britons drank themselves past the fighting stage, and most of them fell asleep. The boys thought this was their opportunity to rescue Merrit, who lay on the ground, still bound hand and foot and apparently forgotten by the Britons.

He must have been terribly stiff and faint from hunger and thirst, for no-one had loosened his bonds or gone anywhere near him since his bearers threw him roughly on the ground when they first came into the village. Bartlett, Berry, and Crossley stole cautiously to the gate, but it was tightly fastened. By standing on each others' shoulders, however, they managed to get up to the top of the palisade, and Berry dropped lightly on the other side. The boys' luck was out; in the darkness, Berry dropped down, not on to ordinary ground, as he had expected, but on to a lean, grey, half-wild dog which lay stretched out asleep at the foot of the fence.

The animal leapt like a tornado into the air, snarling and snapping, and with one flash of its teeth tore the seat out of John Berry's trousers. But the serious part was the noise the dog made aroused the sleeping warriors who were scattered around, and they rushed up to see as well as they could in the darkness what it was that had disturbed the dog. Berry picked up something that came to his hand on the ground, and found it to be a hammer; he swung it at the dog, which had gone for his throat, and was lucky enough to stun it. Then he dived into a pile of straw and leaves, throwing them over him. The Britons scuffled about for some time in the darkness, and twice one of them fell over the very heap of straw which concealed John Berry; but they did not find anybody, and they finally decided that the dog must have had a dream that made it bark. Accordingly, they went back to their interrupted sleep; but the last one, before leaving, casually thrust a spear into the pile of leaves where John Berry was hiding, and the sharp point cut open his leg; but the boy made no sound.

Half an hour passed before all the Britons were asleep again, and Berry was able to move at last; he crept stealthily from his hiding-place and edged along the palisade towards the gate. Though the gate was only fifty feet away, it took John half an hour to reach it, for he had to step carefully over sleeping men, whom he could hardly see in the darkness, and he dared not make a sound. At last he gained the gate, cautiously stepped over the sleeping guard, and opened it. The boys stole in, Crossley carrying the knocker in his hand, for their plan was to grab Merrit, without unbinding him, knock with the Magic Knocker, and all rush through the door before the Britons could recover from their surprise. But once again their plan was wrecked. Just as the first faint greyness of the coming day appeared in the eastern sky, a Briton arose and sounded a queer sort of horn which he had. The boys, who had not yet reached Merrit's side, flung themselves on the ground behind a near-by hut. The strange echoes of the bugle-call rang through the village, and to the dismay of the boys all the people rose, gathered noisily and with much excitement, and marched out of the gate, carrying Merrit in their midst, while the schoolboys crouched trembling behind their hut.

When the last Briton had left the village, the boys thought it was safe to follow; there was little danger that they would be seen, for when they overtook the straggling band of Britons they were in a dense part of the forest, where the dim light did not penetrate at all. The journey was very short. In less than half an hour they emerged from the wood into a great open clearing. Here was an impressive sight. The light was now stronger, though it was not yet day, and it showed them a great ring of stones, taller than houses. The Britons were pouring into the space enclosed by these stones, and standing there very still, facing the east. Here, in the most easterly part of the circle, where everyone was looking stood a grey stone altar.

The scene recalled most vividly to Edgar White a picture he had seen lately.

"Gee!" he said. "Stonehenge!"

Tall bearded men in white robes which swept down to the ground stood by the altar, each with a silver knife shining in one hand and a bough of mistletoe in the other. They were singing a weird blood-chilling hymn, whose sound was ghostly and horrible in the thin light. The boys watched in breathless silence. They were at the western end of the temple, so none of the worshippers could see them, being all too intent on the dreadful ceremony by the altar. Soon the boys saw a stir among the Britons, and then Merrit was carried through the throng of worshippers to the altar and unbound. Now there appeared behind the altar a group of men who dressed like those who stood before it.

The very edge of the land shone like fire

They were carrying a basket woven of rushes, and they were followed by boys and girls clad in white robes, and all singing their horrid hymn. The oldest of the men priests, with their beards flowing down over their chests, now turned to their silent worshippers and said something to them.

"I know what they are," said Taylor; "they're Druids."

"Sh," said Hope, "it doesn't matter much what they are, we've got to get Merrit away from them."

Now the sacrificial hymn was taken up by all the Britons, and its dreadful threatening sound filled the air, while the singers swayed from side to side, maddened by their own voices, their eyes fixed on the Druids and on the boy they were about to kill. Two of the priests were holding Merrit's arms and two his legs. Now they lifted him, and put him into the great rush basket, which had been put down before the altar. The lid was shut down, and still singing, the priests raised the basket and laid it on the altar, on a pile of wood cut from the trees. Now the grey light was brightening in the east; through the opening between two great stones behind the altar the sky glowed redder and redder; dawn was approaching. The hymn rose ever louder, in great waves of fearful, fascinating, hungry music, unlike anything the boys had ever heard. Brighter glowed the eastern sky, and the very edge of the land shone like a line of fire, liquid and molten in its brightness, dazzling to the eye—and still the sun had not appeared. Suddenly at the western end of the

57

temple came a flash of fire. The boys spun round to look; it was a priest, bearing an immense blazing torch. He ran down with it through the crowded Britons towards the altar. The crowd watched him with staring eyes now—shouting, screaming their hymn.

"Quick," hissed Hope, and the boys raced round the outside of the temple. They came up behind the altar, but even as they did so the sky blazed with a crimson light, and the red edge of the sun itself appeared above the land. It was the signal. The Britons howled in frenzy, the priests raised their arms to the rising sun, and the one who held the torch, gaining the high altar, thrust the blazing wood among the wood beneath the basket. The wood and the basket flared up in a second, from the basket came a shriek of terror and pain, drowned almost in the mad chanting of the priests, and at the same moment the boys poured in upon the priests and raced up to the altar.

There was a terrible shout from the Britons.

"Back!" screamed the priests.

Crossley knocked twice on the stone of the high altar, and at the clatter of the Magic Knocker the door sprang into view with a blinding light.

Taylor, Glover, and Martin jumped up on to the altar and dragged Merrit from the blazing basket. At the same moment Mr. Rocket's head appeared through the Magic Door. "About time you were back, too," he said. "Morris I want you to clean the blackboard."

The boys rushed headlong through the Magic Door, leaving the amazed Britons behind them.

Merrit's jacket was still alight as Martin and Taylor hustled him through into the classroom. Crossley tore off the Magic Knocker, and they had one glimpse of the Winged Boy as the door slammed behind them.

CHAPTER V
THE WALL OF DEATH

As you would expect, it was some days before the boys used the Magic Knocker again. Their adventures among the Romans and Britons had left them all a little bruised and sore. Morris had to have two stitches in his head, while Jack Crossley carried the marks of the wolves' teeth in his arm for a long time. And apart from anything else, there was a row about Gordon Merrit's suit, which was so badly burned on the Druids' altar that nearly all of Gordon Merrit could be seen through it, which made him very shy. So all the boys set to work with paste and scissors and made him a suit of brown paper, which he wore when he went home, and in which he looked very striking but not at all human.

However, at the end of rather more than a week the desire for adventure began to rise once again in the boys' hearts. This was strange, because Mr. Rocket was giving them an enthralling lesson on the pence

61

table; but there it is. There's no accounting for boys; you think out the most exciting and stirring things for them to do—such as nouns and verbs, and subjects and predicates, and imports and exports, and poems about Playing the Game—yet they don't like them. It's just sheer contrariness, that's what it is.

Anyway they had quite an argument with Mr. Rocket, who said that they should stay and finish the pence table, and then learn 'Lord Ullin's Daughter'; but in the end Mr. Rocket had to give in, and Jack Crossley set the knocker against the blackboard and banged. The door appeared, dazzling as ever; it opened, and the Winged Boy came through, and trod right on Leslie Rodd's rabbit.

I forgot to mention that Leslie Rodd had brought his rabbit to school. It was a very well-bred rabbit, polite and good-natured. It was almost entirely white, except for the odd spots here and there, and it had thoughtful pink eyes. It hardly ever smiled, but it would fold back its ears when among friends; and when in very distinguished company—titled people, millionaires, and poets—it would twitch its nose very rapidly and for a long time. The boys had spent some time that morning sitting in a ring round Leslie Rodd's rabbit, talking to it, and discussing whether it could be any relation to the White Rabbit in *Alice in Wonderland*. They decided it was no relation, because the White Rabbit in *Alice in Wonderland* was not a real rabbit, but only a made-up one in a story, whereas Leslie Rodd's rabbit was clearly a real one, since you could see it and stroke it. Leslie Rodd's rabbit, further, had no gold watch, nor had it a pocket to put its gold watch in; and all the boys were certain it was better to have a real rabbit without a pocket and without a gold watch in the pocket which it hadn't got, than to have a pocket and a gold watch on a rabbit that wasn't real.

"Oh, I'm so sorry," said the Winged Boy when he trod on Leslie Rodd's rabbit.

The boys thought Leslie Rodd's rabbit would be offended, but it gave one of its rare smiles, and laid its ears back to show there was no ill-feeling. Thus the incident passed off without any unpleasantness.

"Well, how do you like going into history?" asked the Winged Boy.

"Not so bad," said the class, "but we're taking some sticking plaster with us this time." Hope, who had been elected leader of the party, had a big roll of sticking plaster in case anyone was wounded or bitten again.

The boys were already filing through the door.

"Look after my rabbit," said Leslie Rodd to Mr. Rocket. However, the Winged Boy was doing that. He and the rabbit got on very well; you would almost think they knew each other. The Winged Boy sat down at Alec Baker's desk, with the rabbit on his knees, while Mr. Rocket stretched himself out with his feet on the blackboard ledge; and as Jack Crossley disappeared and pulled the door closed behind him, peace settled on the classroom.

As the door slammed behind the boys, and vanished, they saw around them a different scene from any they had expected. They were standing on a stone floor in a large round room, whose walls were also of stone. Instead of windows, there were long slits in the walls, running from near the floor to the ceiling. The entrance to the room was through a tall but narrow arched opening in the wall, and immediately through the opening the boys could see a narrow winding staircase, by which you could go either upward or downward from the room they were in. From this spiral stair came curious and sinister sounds—the shuffling of feet on stone, clashes as of metal, sudden gasps, a shout, and then a groan. Leonard Jackson ran to the stairs to look. Just as he got there, there was a clatter, and an armoured man fell down the stairs, rolled past the room where the boys stood, and disappeared from their view in the darkness lower down.

Grey ran to one of the slits in the wall to look out. From what he saw he began to understand the kind of place they were in. The room in which they stood was one of the floors of a round tower; from this tower, at either side, ran a thick high wall of stone, wide enough for a car to run along. In the distance at either side Edward Grey could see other towers like their own, set in equal spaces along the wall, perhaps a mile or more apart. They were, in fact, in one of the watch-towers of the Roman wall which Agricola and Antonine built to protect Britain from the Picts and Scots. Beyond the wall, almost as far as the eye could see, were trees, not stretched over a plain, but at different levels, some high on hills, others clustered in valleys; and above them, in the farthest distance, loomed the peaks of mountains. All around the watch-tower, and along the wall on either side, were thousands of painted hairy savages, looking far fiercer and more terrible than the Britons had looked. They were shouting their battle cries and waving their spears and hammers above their heads. Some were chopping down the tall trees so that they fell leaning against the wall. Then they climbed up them and leapt on the wall with a shout of triumph. Every now and then one of the savages fell, with a Roman arrow through him; but judging by the fewness of the arrows, there did not seem to be many Romans left.

At this moment a Roman entered the room. At first he did not see the boys at all, which was not surprising, since his eyes were filled with blood from a cut in his forehead. But when he wiped the blood away, sighing as he did so, he saw the boys, and said: "What are you? Where have you come from?"

"We've come a long way," said Bartlett, and started to explain, but the Roman wasn't listening.

"What's happening?" said Edgar White. "Are the Romans losing? Why doesn't Julius Cæsar come and help you?"

"Cæsar? *Julius Cæsar*? Would in Heaven that we had Julius Cæsar to help us now—we never needed him more," said the soldier, in a tone of profound sorrow and despair.

"Then why doesn't he come?" asked Maurice Lane.

The Roman looked at him strangely. "I don't know whether you are mocking a poor Roman who is near his death," he said; "anyway, I don't care now—it is too late. Julius Cæsar would have to come back from the Country of the Gods if he were to help us now. He has been dead for over three hundred years. Ah, how he would weep to see what we have made of Rome since he fought for us. The Empire is falling—falling. It is no more use to pretend; these are the last days of Imperial Rome. The savages are at our gates. The mother city herself, She of the Seven Hills, the Queen of Tiber, is on her knees before her enemies. We can hold them back no longer. The black tide is rising, the shadow is coming on the world. One after another our armies have been recalled to Rome, one after another they have perished, and the great horde of the Barbarians has passed over their bodies. And when herself pants and weakens beneath the hammer blow of her foes, what hope have we, a mere handful of men left here to guard the Empire's farthest outpost? How can a few hundred men hold this wall against all the savages in Caledonia? Our sun has set; but the Scots shall not cross this wall while I live."

Just then there was a scuffle on the stairs, and a cry for help. The Roman ran for the doorway and climbed up about seven stairs. Then he stopped. The boys could still see his legs, but the rest of him was hidden by the arch of the door. He seemed to be struggling with something higher up on the stair. He panted and shifted his feet to stand more firmly, and then suddenly his struggles ceased. His legs crumbled beneath him, and he fell like a log down the stairs. Then a painted savage appeared in the doorway, wounded and streaming with blood. He held a knife between his teeth, and carried in is hand a sword taken from a Roman. Other Picts and Scots crowded behind him, and followed him as he leapt into the room, his cruel eyes fixed on the boys. They ran to the other side of the room, terrified, except for Black, who had his knife in his hand, and threw it with all his force at the nearest warrior. Unfortunately it did little damage, but only infuriated the man. He bared his teeth and ran forward on to Black, with both his hands outstretched. Quick as a thought, Crossley knocked on the stone wall. The man who was about to slay Black sprang back and fell to his knees; all the others followed his example, as the green metal door blazed out of the solid stone. There was a cry of terror from the murderous Picts and Scots, and a prayer for mercy, but the boys were not waiting to listen to it. They scrambled madly through the door . . . and now it would be as well to go back a little, and find out what had been happening in the classroom while they were away.

. . . . . .

As the boys had gone through the Magic Door, the Winged Boy sat down in Alec Baker's desk and said to Mr. Rocket:

"Did you ever keep rabbits?"

"Well I had one once," said Mr. Rocket with a sigh, "but it died"

The Winged Boy sighed too. "They all die," he said, "that's the worst of living for ever. Everything else dies. It isn't only rabbits. Dying is a thing that seems frightfully common. Nearly everybody does it, sooner or later—but rabbits perhaps are more inclined to die than most things. That's because they're born so often. Now I've kept rabbits in my time—many rabbits. To tell you all the rabbits I've kept would take up years. And it isn't easy for me, you know, keeping rabbits, because I'm always being called away into a different period of history, and often I don't get back for a hundred years or so, by which time the rabbit—well, you understand."

Mr. Rocket nodded sadly. "I understand."

"I had a little grey rabbit in the time of George the First," went on the Winged Boy, "but then somebody knocked on the door, and away I had to rush into the time of William the Conqueror. Well, of course, by the time I got back to George the First again, my little grey rabbit—dead. And that was when I decided to have a rabbit in every age, and call them all Henry, so whatever age I happened to be in, I would always have a Henry to play with and feed, even if it wasn't always the same Henry. But it didn't work."

"Why not?' asked Mr. Rocket.

"Well it was feeding them I couldn't manage. Just think of it. I had nine thousand and seven rabbits to look after altogether, and I'd no sooner fed one than I had to dash off a couple hundred years or so and feed another. Dreadful it was. And King George's one fell ill—I remember that very well—his coat came off in patches; and while I was attending to him, Boadicea's Henry ate his way out of the hutch and got lost, and after that I fed King James's Henry three times by mistake, and he burst, so you see—"

At this moment there was a knock on the classroom door, and in walked an inspector.

The Winged Boy darted under the desk like lightning, and as the inspector was rather short-sighted, he did not notice the movement. Mr. Rocket hastily got out his record book and lesson notebook and anything else he could find that looked like work, and opened everything to the page with the best writing on. He also pushed out of sight a half-sucked acid drop and a copy of *Beano*, with which he was in the habit of passing the weary hours. Then he jumped to his feet and began to do his best writing on the blackboard.

As for Leslie Rodd's rabbit, it walked gravely across the floor and tried to climb in to the wastepaper basket.

"Now, boys," said the inspector, "I'm glad to see this is a nice quiet class—er—er—um—bless my soul. Is there anyone here?"

"There's me," said Mr. Rocket meekly, writing out the pence table.

"But—er—my goodness," said the inspector; "where are all your boys, Mr. Rocket?"

"I don't know," said Mr. Rocket.

"You don't know? YOU DON'T KNOW? What do you mean? How dare you don't! I mean, how don't you dare! I mean how do you do?"

"Nicely, thank 'ee," said Mr. Rocket.

"But—but—but—this is preposterous. What does it mean? I can't understand. Have you the cheek to stand there and tell me you don't know where the boys are? It isn't right. It won't do. I won't have it. Once and for all—where are the boys?"

"I haven't the slightest idea," said Mr. Rocket, smiling to show the inspector he shouldn't get worried. "It is most upsetting, inspector, isn't it? But there; I suppose it's all for the best, don't you think?"

"Think? Think? THINK? I can't think. My brain's reeling. Do you mean to tell me you've lost them? Lost a whole class of boys? Where on earth have they gone? Did they come to school this morning? When did they go? For goodness' sake say something; don't stand there grinning like a crocodile and saying, 'I don't know.' Let me tell you this is a very serious matter. Where are they?"

"You know inspector, I do wish you wouldn't keep asking me that," said Mr. Rocket. "If only I knew where they were, I'd be very glad to tell you, because I think it would make you happy; but I don't know. All I know is they went through a door in the blackboard, and I don't know when they'll be back. If you want to wait for them, I should sit down if I were you."

The inspector was much more annoyed by this explanation than he had been before. "Nonsense; rubbish; pooh; bah; absurd; ridiculous; silly," he said. "Door in a blackboard—never heard such a tale in my life—perfectly good blackboard—solid blackboard— no adventure about this blackboard—nothing exciting, no thrills, no romance, no games about this blackboard—never get anywhere with this blackboard."

"Yes, I know, inspector, it's just a board; black and dull—very black and very dull. It has nothing to do with life, excitement, fun, peril, or joy. It doesn't grow leaves in the spring, though it did once when it was a tree—but now we've killed it and made it black and square and dull. It doesn't take the boys on any magic carpet rides into the Arabian Nights. It doesn't bring them the wonders of the deeps or the wonders of the stars. It stays still right in front of them—very square, very black, and very dull—the boys have to sit and look at it five hours a day, five days a week, for nine years, so that they will be good men when they grow up, and will not grumble if the world itself is very square, very black, and very dull. Only this time something's gone wrong, and the adventure has actually come in by that black board. As a blackboard, from now on, it's a failure, inspector—you ought to send it back. It's turned into a gate into the land of

Heart's Desire. That's why the boys aren't here now—they're all gone into the world of light, you see, and I alone sit lingering here."

"Rubbish; nonsense; bah; pooh; tommyrot; twaddle; drivel; absurd; ridiculous; soft," said the inspector. "Magic, indeed, in these days of science. Perfectly good blackboard, I repeat. I believe you've sent your boys home, Mr. Rocket."

"If you won't believe me," said Mr. Rocket, "just look under that desk."

The Winged Boy popped up. "You *would* give me away," he said to Mr. Rocket. "Now if I'm not careful they'll try and cut my wings off and make me go back to school and learn how many ounces in a mile and all the rest of it."

"I should think we will send you to school," said the inspector sternly. "Little boys can't be allowed to do as they like, you know. That's one of the most important things you learn at school."

"But why can't they do as they like?" asked the Winged Boy.

"Well, of course they can't. It would be very wrong of them. They have to do as they're told."

"But who tells them?"

"We tell them—teachers and inspectors."

"Well, then, you must be doing as you like. Why is it right for you to do as you like, but wrong for boys to do as they like?"

"Well it's training for boys, you see—they can do as they want when they grow up, but they have to learn to do as they're told when they're boys."

"But what's the use of learning to do as they're told, if when they grow up they are going to do as they like? And how can they do as they like, if they never had any practice when they were boys?"

"Well, when they grow up, they don't *really* do as they like even then. You see, even I, an inspector, have to do as I'm told."

"But if nobody ever does what he wants to do, what's the good of being alive?"

"Oh, you are a most difficult little boy. You must learn not to argue with your elders," said the inspector; "That's another thing you ought to go to school for."

The Winged Boy was furious. His wings fairly bristled with rage. "Elders, indeed," he said. "I'd like you to know I'm just a million years old, which makes me a bit older than you, and if it's wrong to argue with your elders, you'd better shut up."

It was at this moment the boys returned. There was a terrific bang on the blackboard, and Mr. Rocket said, "There! Who said there wasn't a door?" The inspector looked, and saw a shining green door appear in the middle of the blackboard. He saw the door open and the boys come tumbling through; and he saw a pack of very bloodthirsty looking savages, beyond the door, fall on their knees. Then all the boys were back, and the door was closing.

"Well, well, well; very strange indeed," said the inspector. "Very queer. I shall have to report this to the Education Committee. I think we'd better have that door bricked up."

"It can't be done," said the Winged Boy. "The Magic Door can open in a mountain side—in solid rock. It could almost open in Mr. Rocket's head. You can't brick it up."

"Well you ought to do something about it," said the inspector. "We can't just have the class walking out like that. Where does the door lead to?"

"Oh, somewhere in history," said Jones airily, as if it were no more to go among the Ancient Britons than to go to the fried-fish shop for a twopenny haddock and pennyworth of chips.

"Then all I can say is if the class won't stay with the teacher, the teacher ought to go with the class," said the inspector. "If you boys are going through the door, Mr. Rocket should go as well, to see that you have your lessons just as if you were in school."

"Well—er," said Mr. Rocket nervously—he had nerves of steel, of course, but they were a bit springy.

"Er—I'm not sure that I want to go. I don't want to have arguments with wolves and soldiers, and things like that. I'm alright where I am, thanks."

"But what about lessons?" said the inspector. "The boys have to have their lessons, wherever they are."

"Oh, have they?" said Mr. Rocket. "Well, if I'm going into history, I'm keeping jolly close to that knocker, let me tell you. Crossley, if I have to come through the door with you, you stay where I can see you—understand?"

"Yes, sir," said Jack Crossley.

CHAPTER VI
ANGLES, SAXONS, ET CETERA

"Please, sir," said Bartlett, "can we go through the door today?"

"Yes, sir; let's" said Hope.

"McManus, bring out that paper aeroplane and drop it in the wastepaper basket," said Mr. Rocket firmly; "and as for you, David Rogers, if I see you whispering to Lowther again, I shall certainly murder you and thrust your body behind the blackboard. No, Bartlett, we cannot go through the door today. We have to do some geography today. We have to learn about the density of pop."

"Please, sir, what is pop?"

"Population, of course, you stupid boy,"

"Oh,"

The class had thought it meant something quite different. They were in the bad habit of calling Mr. Rocket 'Pop,' and though they knew Mr. Rocket was pretty dense, they never expected him to give a lesson on his density. If it only meant population they weren't interested.

"Can't we do geography on the other side of the door?" asked Taylor.

"Don't call out, Taylor," said Mr. Rocket. "Hands up the boys who want to go through."

Of course every hand went up. "All right," said Mr. Rocket with a sigh. "I suppose I shall have to give in. Take your atlases and carry then under your arms. Come on Crossley, do your stuff."

Crossley did, and the door opened. "Hallo, folks," said the Winged Boy, flying out like a swallow and circling round the classroom. "I wondered when I should be seeing you again. Do you think this will bear me?" and so saying, he alighted on the gas bracket. It was a very old school and had gas brackets.

"No," shouted Mr. Rocket; "come off it, quick!" but he was too late. As soon as the Winged Boy put his weight on it, the gas bracket came down, bringing with it nearly half the ceiling. "Heads below!" shouted the boys, ducking under their desks, while great lumps of plaster fell on the floor. There was a strong smell of gas.

"Gas-masks, boys," said John Berry.

"You've done it now," said Mr. Rocket to the Winged Boy. "Now you'd better get on mending that while we're gone, else there'll be a row. Make a good job of it, and sweep the room when you've finished."

With these words, the great teacher strode through the Magic Door, and all the boys strode with him.

78

The first thing Mr. Rocket did when he came through the Magic Door was to sit down with a bump.

"Ow," he said, "where am I?"

At that moment Merrit came through the door and fell right on top of Mr. Rocket. Thoughtless of him. Then Glover fell on Merrit, Morris fell on Glover, and Smith fell on Morris. Then all the class fell on them.

Then they all rolled about from side to side as if they were in a swing, and when at last they picked themselves up they were covered in bruises and their clothes were torn. Mr. Rocket, who was right at the bottom of the heap, was squashed flat as a pancake. He is still rather narrow from front to back because of it. He thinks if it had been Standard Seven instead of Standard Three on top of him, he would now be able to go into a classroom without opening the door.

"Hum," he said, taking a deep breath. "If this is history, it feels like a grand piano."

They were in a long narrow ship, manned by many oarsmen. Somehow they had never expected to be in a ship, and Carter had walked right over the side. One of the men had immediately fished him up again with an oar, and now he sat in the stern, all wet dark and shiny, like a half chewed blackcurrant pastille.

In the bows of the ship stood a tall man who seemed to be the captain, since he was giving a lot of orders; in the stern, near Carter, a steersman was holding a rudder-bar—Mr. Rocket would have called it a tiller, only he didn't know that was its name. All the men were tall and broad, with long fair hair and blue eyes. As they rowed, the powerful muscles stood out on their chests and shoulders. Their faces were fierce and cruel. Though the men were dressed in skins, most of them had a certain amount of armour, and the captain wore a tunic of mail. All wore helmets, generally with two horns sticking forward, which made them look extremely savage. The sea was very rough; the boat was rolling and pitching heavily. Mr. Rocket, unable to stand without assistance, wrapped his arms fondly round the mast, as if it were more than a brother to him, while the boys sat down on the floor of the ship, knowing that once they were down they could fall no further.

"How did you get here?" shouted the captain in a voice like a foghorn.

"Magic," gasped Mr. Rocket, hugging the mast grimly as the boat rocked and heaved like a mad horse.

"Oh," said the captain, as if he were quite used to people appearing and disappearing by magic. "Oh. Well maybe you can tell us the way to Britain."

"Sure," said Mr. Rocket, holding on with his legs as well, as a wave nearly carried him overboard; "first on the left and keep right on."

"Are you certain?" asked the captain doubtfully.

"Well, not dead certain," admitted Mr. Rocket. "I'm a stranger in these parts myself. Ask the boys."

"Port your helm," cried Baker.

"Hard a-starboard," said White.

"Take a turn round your winches," said Martin.

"Put a reef in your top-gallants," said Black.

"Furl your deadlights," said Leslie Rodd.

"Strike your colours," said Merrit.

"Fasten your bootlaces," said Lowther.

"Pull your socks up," said Norman.

The captain looked bewildered. "I don't understand," he said.

"What a pity," said Mr. Rocket, "it would be so helpful if you could only understand. But never mind. We were just going to have a geography lesson, so if you will sit down with the boys and look over an atlas with them, you'll soon pick it all up."

"Good," said the captain, and sat down between White and Norman, who edged away nervously from him.

"Now," said Mr. Rocket, still hanging on to the mast, "where are we?"

"That's what I want to know," said the captain.

"Well it's no use going on if we don't know where we are," said Mr. Rocket. "Geography isn't any use if you don't know where you are?"

"But I thought you were doing this geography to find out where we were?" said the captain.

"Oh, no. In geography, you have to know where you are. Then geography tells you were every one else is."

"But I don't want to know where everybody else is," shouted the captain—he was a very short-tempered man. "I want to know where *we* are."

"All right, don't shout," said Mr. Rocket. "Where were you the last time you knew where you were?"

"We left Jutland the day before yesterday, and goodness knows where we've been since then."

"Jutland?" said Mr. Rocket. "Are you Jutes, then?"

"Jutes?" said the captain scornfully. "I should just think we are not! We're Angles, true-blooded Angles and proud of it!"

"ANGLES!" said Jack Morris with joy, and throwing himself at the feet of the captain, he said: "You are my great-great-great-great-great-great-great-great-great-great-great-great-great-great-grandfather— at least, you might be."

"Oh, but I'm not," said the captain in some alarm. "How old do you think I am? Why it would take hundreds of years for anybody to be all that."

"Yes, it did," said Jack Morris.

"Say," said the captain to Mr. Rocket, "are they *all* barmy?"

"Not barmy," said Mr. Rocket, "just simple."

Just then one of the sailors cried, "Land-ho," and looking forward, Mr. Rocket and the boys saw Spurn Point in the distance.

"What's that?" said the captain.

"That," said Mr. Rocket, "is Spurn Point, and just behind it lies the entrance to the river Humber."

"Good old Humber," said the boys.

"Yes, you certainly must be magic," said the captain, "else, how did you know about that?"

"Big Heap Strong Magic," said Mr. Rocket, to impress the captain.

It was not long before the Angles' boat was rounding Spurn Point, which jutted out into the sea. The boys looked round them, hoping to see the familiar banks of the Humber, so Mr. Rocket took the opportunity to give them a little more geography.

"Now, it's no use looking for the kind of banks which the Humber has in our time," he said. "You can see the south bank all right, where Grimsby will stand—only Grim and the other Vikings haven't come across the sea yet. But the north bank—from where Hull will one day stand, right by the coast—is swampy land now, and the Humber flows over a lot of it at high tide. It won't be dry land till the river has changed its course, and the dykes have been built to keep the water in its place."

"Well, where are the banks of the river?" asked Bartlett; "they must be somewhere."

"They're under the water; it just gets shallower and shallower, until it becomes dry land. For all we know, we may be only floating in about ten feet of water now. Maybe even less. There maybe very little water under us now. We maybe almost aground."

At this moment there was a scraping noise and the boat stopped. "We *are* aground," said the captain, and swore for four minutes in Old English

"Thank goodness the boat's stopped," said Carter as he leaned over the side to be sick.

"You're a fine pilot, aren't you?" said the captain to Mr. Rocket, "you've run us aground."

"Don't be silly," said Mr. Rocket, "you've run yourself aground. How did you expect me to pilot you when I haven't been here for fourteen hundred years?"

"Well, what have we to do?" asked the captain helplessly.

"Wait till the tide rises higher, of course," said Mr. Rocket. So they sat quietly in the boat for a couple of hours, and it came on to rain, and before long everybody was soaked through and miserable. Then the captain looked over the side and began to swear in Old English again. When he had been swearing for ten minutes, Mr. Rocket asked him what was the matter.

"Oh, nothing," said the captain sarcastically, "only you told us to wait till the tide came in a bit more."

"Yes. Very sensible. What about it?" said Mr. Rocket.

"Nothing, only the tide wasn't coming in, it was going out, and now we're high and dry on a sandbank."

They all looked over the side, and sure enough they were high and very nearly dry. There was only about a foot of water over the sandbank beneath the boat. The boat was stuck deep into the sand. It looked as though gunpowder wouldn't shift it.

The captain, who was short-tempered, as I have said, made a rush for Mr. Rocket.

"Hoi, what's the game?" said Mr. Rocket, kicking the captain in the stomach.

"I'm going to sling you overboard," said the captain, and sure enough he did. Mr. Rocket landed, with a terrific splash, sitting down in a foot of water.

This annoyed him very much, because he had his best trousers on.

"This is what comes of magic doors," said Mr. Rocket, picking himself up all dripping wet. "I'm soaking. I wish the Angles had never come to Britain, then I wouldn't have spoiled my Sunday trousers. I'm going to wade ashore. You boys can do as you like."

"Wait a bit, I'm coming," shouted Rogers, and dived overboard, burying his face in the sand beneath the water. Mr. Rocket dug him out; his ears were full of sand. The others then jumped over, and led by Mr. Rocket they set off wading ashore.

It took them an hour to reach the land, which sloped gently up from under the river. They had not been ashore long before they noticed a movement among the trees. Stealing up quietly, they came near enough to see a little band of people—men, women, and children—collecting pieces of wood.

"Britons," said Merrit, who had not forgotten his narrow escape at Stonehenge.

"They haven't changed much since Cæsar's time," said Taylor.

"That must have been nearly five hundred years ago." said Crossley.

"How do you know that?' asked Fairweather.

"Well, the Angles and the Saxons and the Jutes didn't come to Britain till the fourth and fifth centuries after Christ, and Cæsar came fifty years before Christ. The Angles and the others didn't come till the Romans had all gone back to defend Rome, as they were doing at the time when we were on the Roman wall."

"So those Angles we've just left really are the first English people, just coming to the country," said Martin.

"You can see the difference," pointed out Hope, who was watching the British very closely. "Look, the Britons nearly all have dark hair, but the Angles have yellow hair; and the Angles are taller than the Britons."

By this time, following the Britons through the wood, they had come to the British village, which was on the bank of a small river, just where the river joined the Humber.

"This will be the River Hull," said Mr. Rocket, "and across the water there is the place where the pier will be in fourteen hundred years from now."

"I bet the Britons would be surprised if they could see the New Holland ferry boat come steaming over the water," said John Berry.

"Let's take a Briton back with us," said Leslie Rodd.

"What, back to the boat?"

"No, back through the Magic Door."

"No," said Borden, "he'd be locked up in prison for not having any clothes on."

"Some of them have clothes on," said Leonard Jackson, "animal skins and things."

"Yes, but you'd get locked up if you went for a walk dressed in a rabbit skin," said Edward Grey.

"Well, we could put some clothes on him."

"S-sh!" said Crossley. "Look there!"

They looked, and saw all the Angles they had left in the boat creeping stealthily ashore. As the tide rose again, their boat had at last floated off the sandbank, and they had landed near the British camp. As there was a slight fog after the rain, the Britons had not seen them. The boys kept very silent and watched. The Angles stole silently on the camp, in single file, hidden by the trees; as they came near, the captain saw a British sentry leaning against a tree, a spear in his hand.

The captain of the Angles made a movement with his hand, and the band stopped. Then the captain and another man stole away out of sight.

A minute or so later they reappeared near the tree against which the sentry was leaning, one on each side of him. They crept close very softly, and then, with the suddenness of lightening, the captain jumped from behind on the unsuspecting man and gripped him by the throat. The captain was about seven foot high; the Briton looked like a child in his hands. The Angle threw him on the ground and knelt on his chest, still holding him by the throat, while the other man sprang forward and plunged his sword through the Briton again and again till his struggles ceased. Then the two Angles stood up. In killing the sentry they had not made a sound.

Mr. Rocket could not stand this. He could not have kept his mouth shut for a fortune. This was because he had the heart of a lion, the strength of Samson, nerves of steel, and so on. As the Angles gathered together again, ready to steal silently on the British village, Mr. Rocket strode forward and said:

"Well, you dirty dog."

The captain looked round and saw him. "Oh, it's you again, is it?" he said. "Just you keep quiet, or you'll be a dead man, magic or no magic."

"Pooh," said Mr. Rocket. "Don't you threaten me, my man. People who threaten me get hurt. Do you know, the last man I hit went so far that when he came back his clothes were old-fashioned?"

"Is that so?" said the captain evenly, watching Mr. Rocket very closely.

"That, and worse," said Mr. Rocket. "If you think I am going to stand by and see you slaughter innocent people as you just slaughtered that one, you can guess again. Before you go creeping on that British village, I'm just going to let them know what's on the way."

And raising his voice, Mr. Rocket, assisted by all the boys, shouted as hard as he could, "LOOK OUT, BRITONS! ANGLES COMING!"

"Gee whiz," said the captain, who, as you will remember, was short-tempered. "Give me my battle-axe, Athelstan."

"Drop it now," said Mr. Rocket sharply. "I never fight with battle-axes."

They reappeared near the tree against which the sentry was leaning

"No?" said the captain. "Well, I DO!"

And he drew himself to his full seven feet and advanced on Mr. Rocket, swinging the mighty meat-carver round his head.

"Say, Crossley, got that knocker handy?" said Mr. Rocket quickly. "I don't like the look of this chap."

There was no reply. Looking round quickly, Mr. Rocket saw to his horror and consternation that the boys had deserted him and had run away to look at the British village. He was alone before the furious giant charging madly down on him with a battle-axe!

"Dear me," said Mr. Rocket, "this *is* awkward. I really think I ought to be getting along now." And he dived like a rabbit between the captain's legs, and beat it into the woods.

The captain did not waste time chasing him, but turned back to his men and said: "Come; we must attack the village without wasting a minute. The shouts of those dogs will have warned our enemies, and we must give them no time to arm. Not a Briton must escape."

He was a merciless warrior, the captain. He boasted that he never took prisoners; if his enemies fell into his hands, he killed them immediately. So it was just as well Mr. Rocket was a good runner.

Mr. Rocket was unable to find the boys at first; this was because they'd decided to hide in such a way that the Angles could not possibly find them, and at Hope's suggestion they had torn leaves and branches from the trees, and squatted down on the ground holding the branches pointing upward, so that each boy looked like a bush or small tree. They were absolutely covered with twigs and leaves, and it was impossible to see any of them. Mr. Rocket found them by accident, however, since he was trampling his way through a hawthorn bush, and the bush said "Ow!" and Lowther's face popped up out of it. All the boys were hidden round the entrance to the British village, so Mr. Rocket made up his mind to do the same, and disguised himself as a large wild cabbage, which was not easy, even for Mr. Rocket, who looks something like a vegetable anyway. He had hardly settled down when the Angles appeared, treading very cautiously through the wood. Mr. Rocket looked so much like a plant that they never dreamed he wasn't one, and one by one they all walked over his face, and wiped their feet on him. Then they came to the sentry who stood in the gateway of the village. They tried to creep up on him as they had done on the other one, but this time the Britons were on the alert, and the sentry saw them coming. He shouted a warning, picked up his spear, and sent it clean as a whistle through the nearest man's chest. Then the other Angles were on him, and there took place a terrific combat. Like Horatius defending the bridge, the sentry stood in the gate and fought all the invaders at once; when at last he fell, slashed almost to ribbons, the other Britons in the village had had time to come up behind him, and they went on fighting over his body. Mr. Rocket was so excited that he popped his head up out of the wild cabbage leaves and shouted,

"Go for it, Britons," while Morris also popped up to say that perhaps the boys ought to shout for the Angles, since they were their great-great-great-great-great-great-and so on. But at last the Angles fought their way in, and then the boys heard terrible death-cries from the village; and at last all was silent, except for the triumphant voices of the Angles. Then the Angles came out again, having first set the village on fire. They carried armfuls of plunder, food, and weapons. Of the village that had been so happy and peaceful that morning, tomorrow there would be nothing but ashes; every man, woman, and child was dead. The flames roared higher as the conquerors came out.

Once again the Angles walked over Mr. Rocket, but this time, as the last one went over, Mr. Rocket was unable to resist the temptation: he bit. He bit the man's foot, very hard. The man gave a scream and jumped up in the air, and then fell flat on Crossley, who was disguised as a willow tree. The man fell with such force that Crossley immediately became a weeping willow. He said "Ow," and stood up; the other Angles turned round and looked on with amazement as one by one all the bushes and trees turned into boys, except for a wild cabbage plant, which turned into Mr. Rocket.

"Magic," said the captain; "where's my battle-axe?" and he made a run at Mr. Rocket.

"Of course it's magic," said Mr. Rocket, dodging behind a tree; "keep off, you big flat footed Angle, or I'll bisect you. I'll cast a spell on you, I will. I'll turn you into a lemon, or a ham sandwich, or something.

There's no knowing what I'll do. Quick—that knocker Crossley."

Fortunately Crossley was ready. Bang went the knocker, the door sprang into view, open, and to the astonishment of everybody, the Angle captain, unable to stop himself, ran right through into the classroom. But you could never catch the Winged Boy napping. He was waiting on the other side, and in his hand was the empty hand-grenade which usually stands on the cupboard in Mr. Rocket's classroom. He dealt the captain a blow like a sledge-hammer—and didn't it steady him! The captain fell like a seven foot tree, banging his nose on Rodd's desk; and the Winged Boy, who was as strong as Hercules, dragged him back through the door by his feet and gave him to his men, who were kneeling terrified on the ground.

"Come on, lads," said Mr. Rocket, "come through, before they get over their fright," and the boys ran through into the classroom. Here they were pleased to see the Winged Boy had been busy. He had mended the ceiling, put up the gas bracket, and swept the floor, and everything looked spick and span. It was only some time later when they came to light the gas, that they changed their minds about the Winged Boy's work. When Mr. Rocket turned on the gas tap to light it up, there was a sound like 'Wheesh!' and a cascade of water poured down on Mr. Rocket and all the boys. They could not get back to the tap to turn it off, and had to run out and turn it off at the main; by that time the classroom was a foot deep in water. The Winged

Boy had fastened the gas bracket to the water pipe by mistake. He was no use as a plumber. They knocked at the door and brought him back to do it again, but even then it wasn't a success. He put coloured gas into the pipes, and to this day one of the mantles burns red, another blue, another green, and the last one yellow.

CHAPTER VII
NOT ANGLES, BUT ANGELS

It was a dreary, rainy morning. The boys ran shivering into the schoolyard, and the prefects let them in at a quarter to nine, without waiting for the whistle. Mr. Rocket, who came to school on his bicycle, was soaked to the skin as well as late. He didn't mind being late, for he was used to it, but he did object to being soaked to the skin. It was nearly five to nine when he sploshed into the school, but he nobly wrote '8.45' in the time-book, so as not to let the school down.

When he finally entered the classroom–which smelt of drying clothes which the boys had hung over the radiators—he was greeted by a disrespectful chorus of:

"Good-morning, dear teacher, good-morning to you."

Instead of being annoyed at the impudence, however Mr. Rocket, with his usual forbearance, contented himself with kicking Alan Hope from one end of the classroom to the other. Then he threw the blackboard rubber at him, but the missile whizzed past his head and cracked the picture of the Boyhood of Raleigh—or was it Drake? Mr. Rocket then marked the register. Hardly had he finished when Borden called out, "Sir!"

"What do you want, my lad?"

"Let's go through the Magic Door."

"Can you do long division of money, my boy?"

"No, sir."

"Well, my goodness—don't you *want* to do long division of money?"

"Er—no, sir."

"Strange! Well—er—in that case, I suppose we may as *well* go through the Magic Door."

Here the boys gave three hearty cheers and surged forward to the blackboard. The only casualty was Rodd, who trod on a marble and sat down very suddenly. In a second the knocker was flashing in Crossley's hand. The dull surface of the blackboard vanished, to be replaced by the shining jewelled door, and the Winged Boy opened it and stepped out.

"There's no need to push," he said firmly; "someone's treading on my wings."

Needler jumped away, saying he was sorry, but a bright silver feather lay on the floor. Leonard Jackson picked it up and pocketed it as a keepsake.

"We're going through, we're going through, we're going through," chanted the boys.

The Winged Boy wore a graver look than usual.

"Just a minute, lads," he said. "Stop a bit and listen to me."

They did so.

"I've told you before about the dangers of going into history. Now, from what I've been hearing just lately, you are the kind of boys who run risks. All I want to do is repeat my warning. It seems that one of you was nearly burned alive the other week by Britons. You've been attacked by wolves, Romans, Picts and Scots, Angles, and all sorts of things. I'm sorry to say it, but if you take my advice, you won't go through the door any more."

"We're not taking your advice," said the boys promptly.

"Please yourselves, but don't say I haven't warned you. The Magic Door leads to *real* adventures, you know, and in real adventures people often get hurt or killed. Perhaps you think it's a kind of fairy spell, and whatever happens you will come back safe and sound. Well, it isn't. You aren't the first to go into history. There was a boy who went through the door only a few years ago. He was thrown into a dungeon under a great castle in the Middle Ages, and he never got out again, because he had lost the knocker; that's how you came to find it. How would you like to be shut in a dungeon, and never see your mothers any more?"

"We won't be put in any dungeon," said Merrit scornfully.

"If we were, we'd escape," said Carter.

"We'd cut our way through the walls," said Charter.

The Winged Boy smiled dryly. "Ever tried cutting your way through a fifteen-foot wall with your finger-nails?" he said. "It takes a long time. And what if you should be beheaded? People have been beheaded you know, in history."

"You'd bring us back to life again by magic," said Martin.

"Yes, there you go," said the Winged Boy. "That's just where you make your mistake. You think I have magic enough for anything. Well, I haven't. I'm only the Keeper of the Door. I can let you go through in either direction, but I can't save you from any danger you run into on either side. I can play tricks with Time, because he is my father, but I can't play tricks with Death."

"Who is Death? Do you know him?" asked Morris.

The Winged Boy nodded. "My uncle. A surly, sullen, black-winged blighter—he's never liked me. I don't like him either, he's always frowning and muttering. Once he went into partnership with Time, but they couldn't agree, and in the end he set up a rival business, and he tries to get all my father's customers. He has a big board out side his shop: on it is an inscription, 'When you're tired of Time, try Death.' He boasts that his shop will be open long after Time has had to close down—but that's silly, of course; they will die, as they were born, on the same day."

"And what will happen to everybody on the day that Time and Death both shut up their shops and die?" asked Squeak Morley.

"I don't know. They say that, Death once dead, there's no more dying then; and I have heard that when Time stops, Eternity will begin—when every sorrow you ever felt will be made up to you, and Time's shop will be unlocked, and you will be given back even the things you thought you had lost for ever. Perhaps, they say, the days of your childhood will come back; you will understand the sad times, and be comforted, and the happiest moments will last forever."

"But don't you know *anything* about it for certain?" asked White.

The Winged Boy shook his head. "I don't really understand politics. The old people talk about it, but I'm only a boy, although I'm a million years old. I've heard, though, that there was someone who promised all sorts of wonderful things for you humans on the day when Time and Death both die. He said you will be sevenfold brighter than the sun; no evil will be able to harm you; nothing shall grieve you; no joy shall be lacking to you; all your wishes shall be obeyed in heaven and earth, yes, and in hell. Nor shall your heart ever dream such happiness, but he will give you endlessly and measurably more. But, as for me, I am not a human, and I suppose I shall die on that day."

Corner patted the Winged Boy on the shoulder.

"Never mind, Wingy," he said consolingly, "after all, a million years is a long enough time."

"I bet you could do nearly everything in a million years," said Edgar Grey.

"What about the Magic Door?" asked Glover impatiently. "If we wait here talking, we'll never get through."

"Yes, let's go," said the others, who were a little bored with all this talk, to tell the truth, but didn't like to hurt the Winged Boy's feelings by dashing off. In less than half a minute they were on the other side of the door.

When Mr. Rocket went through the door—last but for Jack Crossley, who had to bring the knocker—the first thing that caught his eye was a cow's tail. It nearly blinded him. In some annoyance he grabbed it and tied it in a knot round the cow's leg, and said: "Keep still, you blighter." The cow said nothing, but stared round at Mr. Rocket with sad wide eyes, while it thoughtfully chewed cabbage stalks. Meanwhile its tail untied itself and flipped up again. This time it hit Jack Crossley in the eye, so it didn't matter.

Mr. Rocket now had time to look about him, and saw that he and the boy's were in a rude farmyard; though the farmyard was not so rude as the boys, who were chasing the goats into the pigsty and the pigs into the goatsty—if that's the name of the place where the goats lived. Suddenly from the pigsty came a shrill cry of fear, a grunt, shouts from the boys—"Look out, he's off," "Whoa, Neddy!"—and like a ball from a canon there shot out from the doorway an immense, dirty, hairy pig, travelling at something like thirty miles an hour, with Corner on its back, clinging desperately to its ears and screaming at the top of his voice. As the pig went down the farmyard like a whippet tank, the figure of a brawny Saxon farmer appeared near the far gate, and he jumped across the pig's path to stop it. For a moment the boys held their breath in wonder. What was going to happen? The farmer was as firm as a rock, and the pig was as unstoppable as a train. What would happen when the irresistible pig met the immovable farmer?

The farmer bellowed, the pig thundered, Corner screamed. Crash! The victorious pig shattered the farmer's defences, broke through his front line, and scattered his forces in confusion. At the last moment the farmer had quailed, tried to retreat, stood with legs astride to let the pig pass through. In vain! The pig smote him hip and thigh; the farmer went up like a rocket and came down on his head. The pig swept on, smashed through the gate, and tore away down the lane with Corner still clinging and still screaming.

For a second the boys stood in awed silence, watching the dramatic departure of Corner on his mettlesome steed. Then with one accord they plunged forward.

"After him, boys!" sang out Hope.

The Saxon farmer, who was just struggling to his feet, went down again like a daisy beneath a football team, and nearly thirty boys passed over him. When they had gone, he rose again, very slowly, and it looked just like a piece of the farmyard was getting up.

101

At this point Mr. Rocket thought it might be as well to keep up with the boys, and he hurried from the farmyard. The last glimpse he had, the Saxon farmer was turning round and round very slowly, pointing upwards with one finger and muttering. Mr. Rocket decided he was counting stars.

Beyond the gate only the trampled mud of the lane showed where the pig and the boys had passed. Mr. Rocket made haste after them, but had an accident at the first corner.

The accident was a Roman officer. It must have been a Roman because of the helmet and the armour and the Roman nose. Mr. Rocket ran into him head first, and they both rolled in a ditch. "Oh, my goodness," said Mr. Rocket, "are we still with these beastly Romans."

This was not fair, because Mr. Rocket had not been among the Romans before.

The Roman never said a word, but picked up his sword and crawled towards Mr. Rocket along the bottom of the ditch, with an evil light in his eye. "Wow! Murder!" croaked Mr. Rocket, and leapt out of the ditch like a frog. The Roman pounded after him, and Mr. Rocket tore back again the way he had come. Rounding the corner, he smote the Saxon farmer once again, and bowled him over like a ninepin. The Roman followed, running strongly, and trod the farmer well down. Mr. Rocket, careless of where he was going, plunged into the pigsty, where, after falling over half a dozen pigs, he found a door on the other side, and came out into the daylight again. Tired of running he picked up a heavy oak beam, and stationed himself behind the door. The Roman soldier came through, and Mr. Rocket beaned him with the oak beam. Without even a grunt the Roman flopped on the ground. In addition to having nerves of steel, Mr. Rocket was very resourceful. He hastily detached the Roman's helmet, his breast-plate, and other pieces of armour, and proceeded to buckle them on himself, after first removing some of his own clothes. Then he put the Roman in the pigsty and fastened the door; and we will leave him busy in this way while we follow the adventures of the others.

The boys had not run far—following the screams of Corner and the grunts of the pig—when these sounds ceased abruptly in a confused yelling and clattering. Both Corner and the pig were out of sight round the bends in the lane, and the boys could not understand what had caused the sudden silence. They pelted on, and ran full tilt into a company of men, mostly Romans, who were holding Corner pinioned by his arms. Of the pig there was at first no sign, but later Bobby McManus caught a glimpse of a dark ponderous body charging across the fields, so evidently the pig had escaped.

The Romans did not waste any time. No sooner had the boys appeared than a voice said, "Get them," and in a twinkling of an eye each boy was firmly grasped by a Roman. Both Romans and boys stood panting for the moment. The boys now saw that not all the band were Roman, and not all the Romans wore armour. In fact, most of them were dressed simply in clothes suitable for travelling; their sandals were white with dust, and every face among them was shining with joy.

"This is a great piece of luck, Clodius," said one of them to another. "The gods are kind indeed to send us so many Saxon boys without our having to search for them."

"Not Saxons, but Angles, I believe," said Clodius, examining Leslie Rodd, whom he happened to have caught. "Thirty of them, and all, it seems, young and healthy. This will profit us greatly in the market in Rome. Boys of the Angle race are fetching a very high price just now, when fair-haired slaves are so fashionable."

Edgar White happened to be standing near a Roman boy who was one of the band. "What's the game, kid?" asked Edgar.

The Roman boy whispered: "I shouldn't really talk to you, because you're only a barbarian, but nobody's looking. You will be taken to Rome and sold as slaves."

The word, 'slaves' made Edgar White's blood run cold, and he was about to burst into tears when he remembered the knocker, and cheered up. "Who are all these people?" he whispered to the Roman boy.

"Most of us are Romans. I am a Roman. My name is Iulus. We are merchants, trading between Rome and Angle-land. We carry all sorts of things to Rome, but we like best to take slave-boys, because the rich people in Rome are always wanting slaves, and they will pay a good price to get them." He looked doubtfully at Edgar White for a moment, and then said: "I'm sorry for you, being taken away from your mother and father like this. But cheer up. Perhaps you'll get a good master when you're sold in Rome, and you might be quite happy."

Edgar White was beginning to be quite friendly with Iulus and had almost forgotten his captivity, when suddenly rough hands seized him and held him firmly, and an iron collar was locked round his neck.

"I say, Iulus, can't you get them to unlock these beastly things?" said Edgar. "We won't run away."

Iulus looked at him sadly. "I'm afraid I can't," he said; "they won't take any notice of me. They always fasten slaves up like this. Besides, you probably *would* run away, you know, if you were free. I know I would. And that would be the end of you, for they would just shoot you with their arrows."

Just then a voice called out "Ready!" and the band moved on. But not far, for it appeared that somebody was missing. The boys could hear the captors arguing.

"Where is Octavius?"

"You ought to know, you were speaking to him last."

"Where on earth can he be?"

"We can't go without him. He might never be found again."

"He said he was going to reconnoiter the district."

"He should have sent a soldier. The captain should not expose himself to danger."

"Can he have lost his way?"

"Where is Octavius?"

"Where is Octavius?"

"Where is Octavius?"

"WHERE IS OCTAVIUS?"

At that moment, while everybody was gabbling, a Roman officer came striding round the corner. He looked remarkably dirty, as though he had been rolling in the mud, but he wore a fierce and determined expression—so far as could be seen through he soil on his face.

"OCTAVIUS!" cried all the Romans, "WHEREVER HAVE YOU BEEN?"

"Never mind where I've been, here I am now," growled Octavius, adjusting his armour, clearly in a bad temper. "Quick march, the lot of you. Confound it! Confound it, I say! Stop! I must be going blind! How is it I can't see you? Come here, the nearest soldier."

The nearest soldier obeyed, trembling.

"Here I am, sir."

"Why is everything so dark? Is there anything wrong with my eyes? Tell me the truth, dog. Have my eyes been struck out?"

"No, Excellency."

"Then tell me, dog; why can't I see?"

"Your Excellency's helmet is back to front. It is covering your eyes."

"Confound it, so it is," said the officer, hastily reversing his helmet.

All this time there had been a stir among the boys who were chained together. It began with a few puzzled frowns, then they nudged each other; they twisted their heads to look. They became more certain every minute; the unmistakable stride, the growl of bad temper, the face beneath the mud, the helmet back to front, the whiskery knees that showed beneath the Roman tunic, the nerves of steel.

"It's Mr. Rocket," breathed Leslie Rodd, Jack Morris, Squeak Morley, and Jack Crossley all together. "It's Mr. Rocket dressed as a Roman officer."

It was.

They had no time for further discussion, for Octavius barked "Quick march," and the whole band moved on, the boys muttering with rage because Mr. Rocket was a Roman officer while they were only slaves.

Just round the corner they came to the farmyard in which they had begun their adventures. Arising from the middle of the yard was a figure which seemed at first to be made entirely of mud. It was the Saxon farmer. He reeled away, making faint noises like a squeaker.

Next they came to the pigsty, and were about to pass it when from the inside came a series of dreadful sounds. First came five or six terrific crashes, like someone battering a wooden wall with a sledge-hammer. The sides of the pigsty bulged, bent, quivered, and shook at each mighty blow, and each blow was accompanied by the squealing of many pigs and their grunting. Then came an immense roar, "Let me *out*! Let me OUT, I say." Then another mighty crash, at which the pigsty trembled, and a bellow, "Oh, where is he? Oh, let me get at him!"

The Romans and their prisoners stopped in horror and amazement, and one soldier fell on his knees and prayed for protection from the evil spirit. His prayers did not seem to be very effective, for out of a hole in the roof of the pigsty flew a turnip which struck the soldier on the head. Meanwhile the yells from inside redoubled in vigour, and now became bloodthirsty: "I'll bite his heart out; I'll tear his kidneys out; I'll rip him open; I'll turn him inside out like a glove." At this the soldier who had been knocked over got to his knees again and began to pray at double speed, while everybody else stood with open mouth, terrified—all except Octavius.

"Well, what have you stopped for?" demanded Octavius coolly. "Move on."

"But—but—but—the evil spirit in the pigsty," babbled the white faced Romans.

"Nonsense. Probably a pig talking in it's sleep," said Octavius. "Get along now, get along."

But just then a thunderous blow shattered one end of the pigsty and out rushed—to the astonishment and awe of the watchers, particularly the boys—a naked man. He had not a strip of clothing on him, but instead he had a layer of mud which seemed to be, roughly, two inches thick. He was a dreadful figure. Fire flashed from one eye—the other was not to be seen, being buried in mud—he clutched a mighty lump of wood in one hand, and threatened to take somebody to pieces and scatter the works all over. On emerging from the pigsty, he looked around him madly, dancing with rage. "My goodness," breathed the boys, "what a fearful sight." Then he saw Octavius. "Yaroo!" he gurgled murderously, and went for him bald-headed. "Keep him off; stop him!" shouted Octavius bravely. His men leapt forward, ready to do battle even with an evil spirit at the command of their officer. The wild and dreadful figure swung its wooden club and knocked one man senseless, but the others all flung themselves upon him, and soon the evil spirit was at the bottom of a heap of forty Romans, all treading on him. Under this treatment it was surprising how quickly the evil spirit calmed down.

When they hoisted him to his feet, the evil spirit made no resistance. He hung in the arms of his captors, gasping feebly and looking very like a squashed banana.

"I say, Clodius," said one of the soldiers, "in a way, the evil spirit looks like our captain Octavius."

"Yes, he is rather like me," said Octavius, coming boldly right up to the evil spirit—who was, of course securely held. "He is a wizard, who has taken on my likeness in order to destroy me. But I shut him up in the pigsty. There is only one thing to be done with him.

He must be thrown three times into the nearest duck pond. Then his magic will be destroyed."

"But I *am* Octavius, you blockheads," shouted the evil spirit to the soldiers.

"Silence, base wizard," said Octavius, hitting him on the head with a spear-butt. This seemed to do the wizard a lot of good, for he did not say anything more, though his one visible eye rolled dreadfully. Seeing what a good effect the spear-butt had, Octavius hit him a few more times, and in the end the one eye stopped rolling. The soldiers then took him to the duck-pond and threw him in three times, which made him much cleaner, though it muddied the duck-pond; and finally, on the instructions of Octavius, they tethered him to a tree, like a goat, and marched away.

It would take too long to tell of all the weary marches the boys had to make before they came at last to Rome. It must be said that, after a stormy crossing of the English Channel, in which they were nearly ship-wrecked, they landed in Gaul, and were marched across the country, in the charge of that great commander, Octavius, through the passes of the high Alps into the sunlit land of Italy.

Many were the adventures they had on the way. There was the time when Octavius had drunk fifty cups of wine and a skin bottle of home-made beer from the hospitable Gauls. On this occasion, Octavius amazed the soldiers in his charge by compelling them to repeat the nine times table—which they had never heard before—until they all knew how many nines in seventy-two. One soldier had to say this table for two whole days without stopping, and when he grumbled Octavius threatened him with the cane. This was the only time in roman history that a Roman soldier was threatened with the cane.

Then there was the time when the boys, tired of marching twenty miles a day while Octavius rode in a litter, decided to escape, and would have escaped and lived in the Alps, had not Octavius gone on his knees to them and begged them to stay with him.

"For," he said, "I shall be so lonely without you boys, and if I go back through the Magic Door without you, I shall certainly get the sack for losing you, and then I shall end my days on the dole." So they gave in and stayed with him. But in the end they reached Rome.

What a sight was the slave market at Rome! There were slaves of every shape and size—sad slaves and gay slaves, slaves who cried out to the buyers they liked: "Buy me, kind gentleman! Buy me, kind lady! Buy me, noble dame!"—and slaves that sulked at the corner of the dealer's platform. There were healthy slaves, strong slaves, and one slave that was so ill he died while the boys were waiting to be sold. If the slave was fat, the slave dealer said he was a fine strong slave who would last a lifetime; if he was thin, he would make a splendid wine-bearer. If he was tall, he was good for something; if he was short he was good for something else. Octavius said the boys were the very first slaves in Rome who were absolutely good for nothing.

"Well," said Octavius to the slave dealer, who was waiting for the boys, "I've brought you a fine lot here. This is the best band of slave boys that ever came out of England."

The slave dealer grunted and looked at the boys coldly. "That's what you say," he said, and picked up Squeak Morley in one enormous hand, holding him by the neck. "What do you call this—a boy?" he asked. "I'll never sell him. Nobody will buy anything so useless and skinny."

At this the other boys began laughing, and they laughed still more when Squeak Morley doubled up his legs and kicked the slave dealer in the abdomen. "Ouch!" said the slave dealer, and dropped Squeak like a hot coal; but the slave dealer did not seem to be annoyed, as the boys had expected. "He's got a bit of spirit, I'm glad to see," he said. If the worst comes to the worst, I can keep him and train him to be a gladiator."

Meanwhile, on both sides of the boys, other slave dealers were doing a brisk trade. One was showing off a great Nubian for whom he wanted sixty sesterces. "Just take a look at these legs," he was yelling, while the great negro, unable to understand a word, stood like a statue, his arms fettered behind his back. "See these muscles," bawled the man, touching the negro's biceps and the muscles on his shoulders; "step up and feel them for yourself, lady. Strong as a horse, and will last a lifetime with care."

Octavius was busy bargaining with the slave dealer to whom he wanted to sell the boys. "No," he shook his head decidedly, "not a penny less than twenty sesterces each will I take for the boys. They are worth that much to me. My goodness, if I wanted I could get a stall myself and sell the boys for more than that. Just look at that Nubian that fellow's selling yonder. Sixty sesterces he's asking, and mark my word he'll get it; and Nubians are common as flowers in May. If a Nubian will fetch sixty sesterces, don't you expect me to sell Angle boys for two a penny. Twenty is my figure, and you're getting them dirt cheap at that."

The slave dealer was quiet for a while; then he spat on the ground. "I'm not buying," he said. "Not at twenty sesterces each; it wouldn't pay me. I'll take half at that price, though, if you'll let me pick my half."

"No, you won't," said Octavius. "I know the game. You'd pick all the good looking ones, and leave me to sell the others for half price. No, they're twenty sesterces each if you buy the lot, and twenty-five each if you take them separately."

"Say," said the slave dealer, "do you think I'm in this business for charity? I'll take this one for twenty." He took Leslie Rodd by the ear.

"Yes, because he has fair hair, you think you'll be able to sell him for sixty," said Octavius. "Oh no, friend, the boy is thirty sesterces to you; but you can have him for twenty if you buy the lot. You people are never satisfied. How much profit *do* you want? Have I to do all the work of bringing the lads across from England, and you fill your pockets out of my labour? It isn't good enough. Look round you. There isn't another Angle boy for sale in the market, and you know how wealthy customers are going crazy over Angle boys just now. You're in the money if you buy just now; your fortune's made, even if you paid double what I'm asking. Have a bit of sense, man. Make up your mind quickly, or I'll take the boys elsewhere. I'll tell you what I'll do, seeing I know you; I'll sell you twenty-nine of them at twenty each, and I'll throw you the odd one in for free. Now, is it a go?"

The dealer scratched his head thoughtfully. "Well," he said, "it's more than I like to give for boys, but I think they seem healthy—I'll do it."

Octavius swiftly produced from his toga a strong leather bag. "Fork out!" he said. The boys had seen this bag before. It was the one in which Mr. Rocket kept all the marbles he had occasion to take from the boys in his class.

The dealer delved into his money-bags, and counted out to Octavius a tremendous number of gold pieces. Octavius checked them in with shining eyes. The boys watched closely, and every now and then there was an argument. "Hoi, you've missed one, Mr. Rocket." "Sorry," Octavius would say, and the dealer would look up at him with a scowl and say, "Huh, *you* don't miss much, anyway." At last, however, Octavius

114

crammed into his bag the last of the five hundred and eighty gold pieces, and was turning away with a shining countenance when he heard a step behind him. He spun round, and came face to face with the Pope.

Pope Gregory was walking in the market-place, as he often did in the late morning. His attendants, robed in rich silks and gold, walked behind him, while two white-clad choristers bore the cross before him. With a level eye the great Pope was taking in all the activity and colour of the market-place—the slaves on their platforms, and the shouting dealers, the crowds who looked round for the cheap stall, and the few nobles who were out to buy the finest slaves they could see; and the old people whose children had been torn from them, who had followed the slavers to Rome, and now wept by the platform as they stood and watched them for the last time. As he passed along, the Pope approached Octavius who was still putting away the last few coins he had got for the boys.

"Sinful man!" said Gregory.

Mr. Rocket looked annoyed. "Sinful yourself," he said. "Who are you calling sinful?"

There was a murmur of astonishment and horror from the Pope's attendants at Mr. Rocket's answer, but the Pope took no notice.

"Base wretch, to sell innocent children for gold," said Gregory.

"Innocent are they?" said Mr. Rocket. "You don't know them."

"Vile creature—reptile," said the Pope. "I will not soil my lips to speak to you."

"Don't you call me names," said Mr. Rocket, going red. "I'm not going to stand it, even if you are Pope Gregory."

"Come here little ones," said the Pope to the boys, taking no more notice of Mr. Rocket. The boys approached, blushing modestly, and stood near the Pope, while the slave dealer, who had fallen to his knees before the Pope, remained in this attitude of prayer, and was heard to mutter from time to time, "You can have the lot, Your Holiness, for eighty sesterces each."

The Pope laid his hands on the heads of Jack Morris and Maurice Lane. "What sweet, innocent little children they are," he said. They smiled sweetly and innocently.

"And what country do they come from?" asked Gregory. "From Angle-land, Your Holiness," said the dealer.

"And what race do they belong to?"

"They are Angles, Your Holiness."

The Pope smiled gently on the boys. "Not Angles," he said "Not Angles, but Angels."

"Oh, no," said Jack Morris. "Angles—that's what we are. It's because of our great-great-great-great-great-grea . . ."

But the Pope was not listening to him. "Angels," he was saying; "not Angles, but Angels."

"That's what you think," said Mr. Rocket.

116

"You can have the lot for eighty apiece," said the dealer.

"I will buy them," said Gregory. "I will buy them, and teach them to be Christians."

"We *are* Christians," said Wilf Charter.

"Eighty sesterces," muttered the dealer.

"Don't you buy them," said Mr. Rocket. "Take my advice, Your Holiness, and don't buy them. The man's a cheat. Why, he only gave me twenty apiece for them."

"Silence, base wretch," cried the Pope. "Would you measure a human soul in gold? Come here, my money bearer, and count out eighty sesterces for each of these boys."

The money-bearer came forward and began counting. It took him an hour; at last the gold was piled up before the greedy eyes of the dealer, and the boys were lined up behind the Pope's attendants to follow him to the palace. It was here that they very nearly lost Mr. Rocket for good. The Pope seemed to have taken a terrible dislike to Mr. Rocket.

"Never have I seen so evil a face," he said, looking at Mr. Rocket. "O trader in children, you deserve to die. You have the look of a snake. You are the most hideous villain I have ever beheld."

Mr. Rocket was very hurt. "It isn't right," he said; "you shouldn't say such things to me. I can't help my face."

"Go, lock him in the lowest dungeon of my palace," commanded Gregory, and at his command two attendants went for Mr. Rocket, and would probably have thrown him into the dungeon if they had caught him. But Mr. Rocket was off like a rabbit, and the attendants soon lost him in the winding streets of Rome. But, unfortunately, they weren't the only ones to have lost him; he had lost himself. Before he had run three streets, he had not the faintest idea where he had started from, or where the boys were; and since the boys had the Magic Knocker with them he was very anxious to find them, in case they should take it into their heads to go back to their own time without him.

Alas! The farther he went the more hopelessly he lost his way. Soon he was in a maze of dark and twisting streets, thronged with ragged soldiers who looked as if they would cut his throat if they thought he had anything worth taking. He trembled and hid his money-bag close beneath his cloak, but his luck was out. Running round the corner he cannoned into a great ruffian, nearly seven feet high, and fell flat on the ground. The leather bag fell too, and lay there on the ground. Out of the neck of it, which was not tied up very tightly, rolled—one gold piece. The seven-foot giant looked at the gold piece, then at the money-bag, then at Mr. Rocket. Mr. Rocket turned very pale, and crawled like a crab over the ground towards the money-bag. When he got to it, he turned. The giant was crawling exactly one inch behind him. Mr. Rocket gave one terrible scream of fright, leapt three foot in the air, and ran as he had never run before; so did the seven-footer. They went like the wind, up street and down street, Mr. Rocket screaming all the time like a cartload of pigs and the giant thundering and growling. Mr. Rocket clutched the money-bag tightly in his fist. Nearer and nearer drew the giant, louder and louder yelled Mr. Rocket, and then—suddenly—they burst round a corner, full among the boys, who were still quietly following Gregory.

"Save me, save me," yowled Mr. Rocket, throwing his arms round Edgar White.

"Quick," shouted Edgar White to Jack Crossley.

'Bang!' went the knocker in Jack Crossley's hand. And half a minute later they were all in the classroom again.

CHAPTER VIII
EXCALIBUR!

GOLD—alas! What is it? We struggle for it, and steal it, and murder for it; but what is it but dirt? That was what Mr. Rocket said to the boys. How true it was! How wise!

But, strangely enough, the boys seemed to think differently, and Peter Fairweather said: "Well, if you think gold is only dirt, why don't you give us our share of the gold you got when you sold us at the slave market?"

"But I *have* given you all your share, every penny," said Mr. Rocket. "I don't know why you boys should be so mean about things like that. As if *I* would cheat you."

"Well, it's funny to me if all that money only works out to one-and-threepence each," said John Berry. "There seemed to be a lot more than that when the man was paying you."

"He swindled me!" cried Mr. Rocket in a rage. "The dirty hound, he only gave me twenty sesterces each for you boys, and he got eighty apiece from Pope Gregory. The lying cheating, four-flushing, hard-backed, double-barrelled, stone-hearted, pilfering, profiteering twister! The low-down, wrangling—"

"Say, if you think gold is only dirt, what are you getting excited about?" asked Black. "What if he did rob you, you don't care about money."

"Don't I, though?—I mean, no, of course, I don't," said Mr. Rocket. "Only, I don't like to be twisted—"

"No, neither do we," said Bobby McManus. "Come on, shell out that money you got for us in the slave market."

"Are you going on about that again?" asked Mr. Rocket. "I've told you till I'm sick of telling you that there isn't any left. I've given you every bit, except the bit I kept for myself."

"Yes; how much was that?" asked Stewart Needler.

"Only one-and–threepence, same as you got," said Mr. Rocket. "I wish you lads would shut up about that money. You know I wouldn't cheat you even if I was starving. I hate greedy boys. The way you go on about the money, anybody'd think there was nothing in the world except money. You've got your one-and-threepence, and it was only my honesty that made me give you that. Lots of folks would have kept it, but I'm not like that. I don't spend all my time pinching and scraping after gold. What is gold, anyway? Dirt. That's what I say. Why, if I were you lads, arguing and quarrelling over a handful of money, I'd be ashamed of myself."

"Look here," said Alan Hope firmly, "if you gave us our share and you kept one-and-threepence, how was it that you could afford that new fountain pen? And the new raincoat you came in this morning? *And* the new car you got the day before yesterday? *And* that pearl tiepin? *And* your new wrist-watch, even if it is only rolled gold?"

Mr. Rocket broke down and confessed. "My boys, I have sinned. I thought you wouldn't know. I didn't— I didn—" he sobbed, "I d-d-d-din't keep m-much, and I w-w-wanted a n-new c-c-ccar ever s-s-so m-m-much. W-w-w-will you forgive m-me?"

The boys looked at him very gravely. "Well," said Carter, "it's a very serious matter. I suppose we ought to tell the police. How much did you keep?"

"N-n-not m-much," said Mr. Rocket; "only t-t-ten th-th-th-thousand p-p-p-pounds."

"TEN THOUSAND POUNDS," said the boys.

Mr. Rocket bowed his head in shame.

"What will you do if we let you off this time?" asked John Martin.

"I'll never do it again," said Mr. Rocket, "and I'll g-give you a ride in my new car."

"All right," said Jack Crossley. "I think we ought to forgive him this time." So they did.

"And now, what about the Magic Door?" went on Crossley.

Mr. Rocket was too humbled to say no, as he usually did—not that they ever took any notice of him—so they knocked and passed quickly through the now familiar door.

"What is it?" asked Baker.

"A waterfall," said Glover.

"A cloud," said Rodd.

"It's non of those," said Corner; "it's a beard."

It was—and what a beard. It was such a big beard that it hid more than half the man that wore it. It was a glorious white beard, fully five feet long. It was worn by one of the tallest men the boys had ever seen. He was a magnificent fellow, for he looked older than the hills and wiser than the stars. His old blue eyes were still sharp as frost, sparkling blue points over the snow of the immense beard. The skin of his face was red and wrinkled like a Cornish apple, and his thin snowy hair swept past his ears to join his splendid beard, as tributaries flow to the river. He was angry, too, there was no doubt about that, and there were things about his anger which made the boys feel quite uncomfortable. He was angry with a group of men who stood close by. The boys now turned to look at those men.

They were knights and nobles, and they seemed as angry as the old man. One was wounded, and stood, pale as death, leaning on his spear. Another lay dead; his blood stained the ground. Two others had been just about to strike each other with their swords, but evidently the old man had stopped them.

The old man was speaking. His fierce white hair and beard lifted in the breeze. "Ah, folly and greed, ambition and vain jealousy!" cried the old man. "Is this a fit thing for the lords of Britain, when the enemy is within our land, and we are into this mountainous corner? Is this the end of the great names of Britain? Are we still Britons, or are we no more than quarrelling dogs, that we slay each other for envy? Beware, ye proud, foolish, nobles, beware the wrath of Merlin!" As he said this, the old man raised his hand, and to the terror of the nobles—and the boys—across the whole expanse of the sky swept the shadow of the old man's arm. "Ah!" cried the old man, raising his voice. "I am an old man, but I am Merlin still. This is the hand that can call the waters from their places, the rivers from their beds, the seas from their shores. Will you defy this hand? This is the voice that can bring the mountains crashing down into the plains. Will you disobey this voice?" He stopped, and an even more amazing thing happened. The echoes of his voice went on, rolling further and further away, but growing louder instead of softer, till they became a rumble of thunder that rolled and clattered on the distant mountain tops.

"What shall we do, O Merlin?" asked one of the nobles timidly, for they were all afraid of the terrible old man.

"You shall listen to my counsel. Are you prepared to do that?"

There was a mutter of agreement from all the nobles. "Yes, O Merlin, tell us what we must do, for we must have a king."

Merlin spoke again. "You were quarrelling and spilling each other's blood to have the throne. What will it be worth, if you kill each other till there are few Britons left; what will it be worth to be king?"

"Nothing, O Merlin. A king is nothing, if his people have slain each other."

"Good," said Merlin; "you are not all mad with greed and ambition, then. Now I will tell you who shall be your king. I shall give you a king. Turn your eyes to yonder hill. What see you beyond the hill, over the top of it?"

"The cathedral, O Merlin."

"The cathedral. Good. Tell me; what is there in the doorway of the cathedral?"

"The Holy Stone, O Merlin."

"And what stands firm in the Holy Stone, O lords of Britain?"

"The sword Excalibur, O Merlin."

"And what is the story of the sword Excalibur, O lords of Britain?"

"It is said, O Merlin, that whoever shall draw the sword Excalibur from the stone in which it stands fast, that man shall be king of Britain."

"Then, lords of Britain, go ye unto the Holy Stone and await me there. There I shall bring you a king, and he shall prove himself your true king when he stands at the Holy Stone." Merlin waved his hand to show that

126

he had finished speaking, and at the wave of his hand a shadow passed again over the sky, and the wind moaned like a beast which he kept in leash. The people hurried away in the direction which he indicated, and the old man walked slowly away in another direction.

His path brought him towards the boys and Mr. Rocket. They could see that, though he got his way with the British nobles, he was still very worried, and they wondered what it was that was making him so uneasy.

"What's biting you, Merlin?" said Mr. Rocket, anxious to be helpful. Merlin looked up at him, seeing him for the first time.

"I am deeply troubled, O stranger," said Merlin. "Here is a difficulty which even old Merlin cannot over-come."

"What is it?" said Lock cheerfully. "Tell us, we may be able to help you."

Merlin looked at the boy for a moment with his strange clear eyes, and then said: "Follow me. It may be you are sent to help me in my need."

The boys and Mr. Rocket followed the old man. He seemed to walk slowly, yet they all found themselves out of breath as they panted along to keep up with him. He led them away from the hill where the nobles had gone, along by a riverside, and close in under a rocky cliff. Then they turned sharply from the course of the stream, into a deep glade in the ground, and this deepened till it became a ravine. Here the murmuring of the water could not be heard, but another sound took its place in the hush. It was the sound of sobbing.

The path turned abruptly, and the boys found themselves in a cool cave, hollowed in the solid blue rock. Here, on a stone ledge in the dimness of the back of the cave, sat a boy, weeping bitterly. He was clad in rich though simple clothes. His appearance was noble. He did not see the new-comers, for his head was bowed in his hands. Merlin stood still watching him, and the boys and Mr. Rocket watched him too.

"What is it all about? Who is this?" asked Mr. Rocket.

The boy looked up at the sound of a voice, and stared at the boys through eyes bright with tears.

"This is Arthur, King of Britain," said Merlin.

"What's he crying for? I wouldn't cry if I was a king," said Dennis Smith.

"Do you know what he has to do today?" asked Merlin.

"Yes, I know," said Edward Grey. "He has to pull the sword Excalibur from the Holy Stone which stands in the gateway to the cathedral."

"Why has he to do that?" questioned Merlin.

"To prove that he is indeed the son of Uther Pendragon, and the rightful king of Britain," said Jones.

"Then ask him why he is crying."

"Why are you crying?" asked Black.

Arthur held out his right hand. The wrist swollen and blue. "I must pull out the Magic Sword this day, and I have sprained my wrist, and can hold no weight."

The boys were horrified. "But can't you even pull out the sword? It will come out easily, by magic," said John Martin.

"Look," said Arthur, "I cannot even lift my small dagger from the floor; how then can I hope to draw the mighty sword Excalibur?"

It was true; he could not lift the small dagger. The boys watched him try.

"But surely," said Mr. Rocket to Merlin, "you can cast a spell on the sword, so that it will not weigh anything? Then he could pull it out."

"Alas!" said Merlin, "that I cannot do. In obedience to my power the sword will come from the stone, but beyond that I can cast no spell on the sword."

"Then let Arthur draw the sword with his left hand," said Eric Taylor.

Both Arthur and Merlin caught their breath in horror.

"DRAW THE SWORD WITH HIS LEFT HAND!" they both gasped.

"Yes. Why not?"

"Impossible," said Merlin. "You don't know what you're saying. Arthur could never be king if he drew the sword with his left hand. Everything he did would go wrong. The nobles would never follow him. There would be no hope at all for a king who first drew the sword with his left hand."

"Well, I don't see what you can do," said Charter.

"Go and tell the people he isn't going to draw the sword today, but he will do it next week," said Rogers.

"Impossible," said Merlin. "You saw how they were fighting before. One of them was killed only half an hour ago. It was hard enough for me to make them stop just then, and if I go to them and tell them that their king won't be chosen for yet another week they'll kill each other in the meantime. They are waiting for us at the Holy Stone. I cannot disappoint them."

"You'll have to disappoint them," said Mr. Rocket.

"What can I do? What can I do?" said Merlin.

"I know," said Arthur.

"What?"

"Come over here," said Arthur. Merlin did so, and Arthur whispered to him for a moment or two.

Merlin shook his head. Arthur whispered again, and slowly a light broke on Merlin's face.

He came back to the boys, took Edgar White by the shoulder, and drew him towards the light. Then he looked closely at his face.

"You are right," he said, turning to Arthur. "Come here."

Arthur did so, and stood by Edgar White. Merlin stood behind them, and draped his long cloak over their shoulders so that it hid their bodies but left their heads showing. "Look," he said to the other boys.

Mr. Rocket and the boys walked round so that they could get a good view, and then they all held their breath in amazement; they could not tell which was Arthur and which was Edgar White. They were so much alike they might have been twins.

"Marvellous!" said Mr. Rocket.

Merlin tilted Edgar White's head back, and his cold clear eyes stared into the boy's eyes.

"You shall be Arthur," he said.

"I? Arthur?" stammered Edgar.

"You. Do not be afraid. It will be easy, what you have to do."

"I won't. If I'm King Arthur, I will have to live at Camelot, and I'll never go back home. I won't be Arthur, so there."

Merlin smiled kindly. "Silly boy. I don't mean you shall be Arthur for always—only for today."

"But I'm not Arthur. The Magic Sword won't come out for me," said Edgar White.

"Yes, it will. Leave that to me. As soon as you grasp the sword, it will slide from the stone as if you were Arthur himself."

"But the nobles will know I'm not Arthur."

"No, they won't. They haven't seen Arthur before, except one or two of them, and *they* will never know, because you are as much like Arthur as his reflection in a still pond."

"But—but—I can't—"

"Yes, you can," said Arthur. "You are my only chance. Don't let me down, Edgar."

"Well—all right then; but you'll have to tell me just what to do and what to say, or else I shall get it all wrong."

"You don't have to say much, so don't worry about that. The main thing is clothes," said Arthur. "You'll have to change clothes with me."

"Better do that now," said Merlin; "then we can get on the way."

In two minutes Edgar White had changed clothes with young King Arthur, and they were so much alike that it was hard to believe it was not Edgar White who now sat with a sprained wrist at the back of the cave. Then Merlin said there was no more time to waste, and all except the king set out for the cathedral gate.

As they rounded the shoulder of the hill, they passed through the outlying streets of the town. Here many people turned out of their houses to watch them, and joined on behind the band, so that soon there was a great crowd of about a thousand people, led by the boys and Mr. Rocket, and with Edgar White and old Merlin right at the very front. All eyes were fixed on Edgar White.

"'Tis indeed a noble boy," whispered all the people, and Edgar blushed. "Ay, and 'tis a goodly knight that strides beside him," they said. Mr. Rocket, who felt, very noble indeed, thought they meant him and was bowing to the people right and left of him; of course, they meant Merlin

They could not tell which was Arthur and which was Edgar White

It was not long before they reached the cathedral gate, and met the British nobles for the second time. It seemed as though the nobles could not go five minutes without fighting; they were at it again. This time they were quarrelling about the Sword. They all thought they could pull it from the stone, and thus prove themselves rightful King of Britain, but none of them would let anyone else have first pull; so, of course, nobody could have a go, since, as soon as one of them laid hold of the hilt of the sword, another one pushed him away, and he wanted first pull. By the time the boys came up the nobles had got to fighting again, and one of them stabbed another just as Merlin arrived. Merlin was so furious that he could not restrain himself, but snatched a sword from the nearest soldier, and with one blow clove the man's head to the chin, so he fell dead by his victim.

The people shrank in horror from the terrible wizard, and he stood, with the dripping sword in his hand, and spoke to them in his rage. But somehow even Merlin himself seemed to have lost some of his power over the nobles, and though they listened to him, they did so with lowered heads, sulkily. When he finished, one of them said: "Show us the king you have brought us, Merlin."

Merlin turned back upon them.

"He is here," he cried, and stooping, he caught up Edgar White in his mighty arms, and lifted him high above the crowd.

There was a howl of rage from the nobles, and Edgar White had a horrid fear that they were about to rush forward and tear both himself and Merlin to pieces.

"What is this, Merlin?" cried one of the nobles, with a wicked laugh. "We ask for a king, and you give us a boy."

"This is your king; Arthur, son of Uther Pendragon," said Merlin.

There was a roar of sound from the crowd, everybody talking at once. "Uther Pendragon never had a son," said some, while others cried, "I am the only son Uther Pendragon ever had" ; "I am Uther's son" ; "I am the only son of Uther Pendragon" ; "I should be king" ; "I am the rightful king" ; "I" ; "I" ; "I."

"SILENCE!" cried Merlin. The shouts ceased.

"Forward, all you who claim to be the true King of Britain," said Merlin; "forward, you shall prove your claims."

Out of the people stepped about twenty nobles, clad in rich mail. They were mighty warriors, though none was quite as tall as Merlin. The first laid hold of the jewelled hilt of Excalibur, the Magic Sword, whose blade was embedded in the granite block at the gate of the cathedral.

"Stop," said Merlin. The noble paused.

"First read to us the words which are written on the hilt of Excalibur, that we may know for certain what it means if any shall pull the sword from the stone."

The man stooped and read the words graved on the hilt:

'Steel in stone what hand shall stir?
Grip shall fail and grasp shall tear:
Yet the Block shall yield the Brand
Kindly to King Arthur's hand.'

Again the noble grasped the sword, and this time he braced his foot against the stone, and heaved with all the force of his mighty shoulders. Slowly all his strength came into play, till his joints cracked with the strain, and his knuckles gleamed white through his bronzed skin; sweat stood on his brow, his teeth set gritted with effort. The sword did not move so much as a hairsbreadth. Still the British noble heaved, groaning with exertion, and then suddenly his grasp slipped from the sword-hilt, and he fell with a thump flat on the ground. No sooner had he fallen than another took his place, eager to try and shift the sword. It was equally vain. One after another they tried, one after another they exerted all their strength, but not one of them could displace the sword the least fraction. At last they had all tried, and there was no-one else who wished to take his place at the stone. Then Merlin said: "Are you satisfied that the rightful King of Britain is not among you?"

"There is no-one here who can move the sword," cried the nobles. "It cannot be moved. No-one can be King of Britain."

"You are wrong," said Merlin; "the sword can be moved. There is one here who can move it, and he shall be King of Britain."

The nobles laughed.

"Dost thou think, O Merlin, that the boy thou hast brought can move the sword, when we mighty warriors have tried and failed?" And they talked to each other, saying: "Merlin is growing old, and in his old age he becomes foolish. To think that a boy of eleven or twelve can move the sword which we cannot shift."

"In truth," said Merlin, "you are mighty warriors, but I give you a king who is mightier as a boy than you are as men. And it is true I grow old, but I am not yet as foolish in my age as you are in your strength. You are mighty warriors, but an old man is wiser than you, and a boy is mightier. Watch!"

In spite of their mocking laughter, the nobles could not help watching. Edgar White strode forward—outwardly careless enough, but inwardly terrified lest the magic should not work—and he laid his hand on the hilt of the Magic Sword. No sooner had he touched it than the queerest feeling ran through him, a feeling he had never had before. The mocking faces before him vanished, and he no longer knew what he was doing, except that he felt he was stronger and bigger than anything in the world. He felt that when he moved his feet he strode over mountains, and the twitching of his eye lid sent clouds blowing over the mountains and shadows running over the sea; the trees nodded when he sighed, and he had only to wish to make whole nations happy. And the strangest thing of all was that at the very touch of his hand, the sword slid in the stone like a hot knife in butter, and without thinking very much what he was doing, he drew it easily forth and pointed it straight above his head—the whole long blade of it shining like frozen lightning. And from the crowd that watched him came a murmur of awe and wonder: "Ah, ah! He is our king indeed."

The nobles who had been so sullen now fell on their knees and begged him to forgive them, and vowed they would serve him faithfully till they died; and all the crowd conducted Edgar White to the palace, and put a crown on his head, and declared him King of Britain. There followed a great feast and much rejoicing, and Mr. Rocket got slightly drunk—but not seriously drunk, just merry.

It was nearly midnight before the people at last left the boys, Mr. Rocket and Merlin to themselves, and Merlin said he would never forget what Edgar White had done for him in taking the place of Arthur. They went back in the still moonlight to the cave where they had left Arthur, and found him asleep. When Merlin woke him and told him what happened, he gave Edgar White a thick gold ring, and thanked him on his knees, which made Edgar feel uncomfortable. Mr. Rocket thought it in very bad taste, however that nobody thanked him—after all, if he hadn't let the boys come through the door, Edgar White would never have been able to take Arthur's place. But there, nobody ever appreciated Mr. Rocket. Then Merlin told Edgar White that if he was ever in danger he had only to call on Merlin and he would be rescued, if Merlin could do it—"And I can do most things," said Merlin. And finally, since all the boys were tired and yawning, they went back through the Magic Door.

CHAPTER IX
THE TRUTH ABOUT ALFRED

"You know," said Arthur Black, not very politely, "It's a pity to say it, but really you are the dullest king in history."

Alfred took off his crown, which he had been wearing to impress the boys, put it down amongst the nettles, and burst into tears. "I don't know how you can be so rude," he said, "I'm sure I've always tried to do my best."

"Of course you did," said Alan Hope, passing the king a very inky handkerchief, with which he wiped his royal eyes. "That's just it, Alfred, old chap. You always did your best, and you never did anything you shouldn't, and never swore and never smoked—"

"He couldn't smoke," interrupted Squeak Morley, "'cos cigarettes weren't invented then."

"Don't interrupt," said Hope. "What I was saying was, that if you never do anything you shouldn't, well,

I suppose it's all very well, but you can't call it interesting, can you?"

Once again the boys were on the right side of the Magic Door—that is, of course, the side away from school and lessons and all the irritating things we have to put up with. This time they had run right into Alfred the Great as soon as they got through the door. He was ambling along in a wood— the boys found the country was mostly woods in those days, and thus much more interesting than it is now. Of course he was disguised as a wandering minstrel, but that didn't deceive the boys. For one thing, he was strolling along, clad in rags and very dirty, reading a large Latin book called *Boëthius*; and while the lads didn't know anything, and very rightly didn't want to know anything about *Boëthius*, they thought it unlikely that a poor wandering minstrel would be able to read Latin. And then Billy Bartlett had seen the golden crown gleaming in a sack which the minstrel carried on his shoulder with his harp. So they quickly surrounded the minstrel, and asked him who he was; and when he saw that they were only boys—apart from Mr. Rocket, who sat down and went to sleep while they were talking—he told them, in a whisper, but with some pride, that he was the King of England.

"Name?" asked Meredith Jones.

"Alfred."

"Oh," said all the boys with disappointment. And then Arthur Black made the rude but, alas, true remark which opens this chapter.

140

"It doesn't seem right to me," said Alfred, wiping away a tear with the corner of Alan Hope's handkerchief, and leaving a long smear of ink across his royal brow.

"It isn't right, that when I've done all I could for my country, I should be insulted in this way. Dull, indeed. Where would England be now if it wasn't for me?"

"I dunno," said Morris, while Cecil Carter was heard to mutter that he thought England would stay in pretty much the same place anyway.

"Well, I'll tell you," said Alfred indignantly. "If it wasn't for me, England would now be in the hands of the Danes."

"Really," said Arthur Black, politely this time.

"Yes, really. It's only because I've built up our army, and worked out our defences, and above all—but, of course, you will have heard of the greatest thing of all, my mightiest achievement?"

"I dunno," said Morris again.

"I created the navy," said Alfred.

"Um," said the boys, not very interested.

"I suppose it doesn't sound much to you," said Alfred, hurt. "It's a grand thing to do, all the same. You see, the ships of the Danes—but let me start at the beginning, so that you can understand all that happened. I don't really blame the Danes for all the trouble we've had. They've been terrible foes to me and my people, but it isn't entirely their fault, in a way. You see, the country where the Vikings come from is

141

over the water to the north-east, yonder—I hear that they call it Denemearc—"

"That's Denmark, lads," said Mr. Rocket, to show the boys he was listening. Then he went to sleep again.

"Well, that country is mountainous and rocky," went on Alfred. "I don't suppose you boys have ever done any farming on rocky country?'

"I once had a holiday on a farm in Wales," said John Berry; "the fields were very stony."

"Yes, that's just it," said Alfred. "you see, the soil isn't very deep in rocky country; if you dig down a bit, you come to rock. And, of course, you can't grow things on rock. So what happened in Denmark and all the other countries round there was that the people grew their food, and reared their families there, on the food they could grow; but, just as the number of people was increasing the food began to go short, because the soil was worn out."

"I didn't know you could wear soil out," said Alan Hope.

"Oh, yes; particularly if it's shallow, as this was," said Alfred. "So the Danes had to find other ways of getting food, and the easiest way was to get it out of the sea—so they turned fishermen; and that taught them to be good sailors. But still they remembered that they were really farmers, and when their ships took them right over the water to England, they looked at the fine fertile soil of the country, and the flowing rivers, and they decided they would like to have the country for themselves. But they didn't really try to take the country at first—they just crept inshore and stole whatever they could, and killed anyone who got in their way. You see, they were just pirates. But after a time they came across in bigger ships, and more of them, and they landed and fought battles with my people, and even built their own camps and forts up in the north. So I had to protect the country. And the only thing I could do, to beat off the Danes, was to meet them *before* they got to England. Clever, don't you think?"

"I would have thought of it," said Mr. Rocket, opening his eyes.

"Maybe you would, and maybe you wouldn't," said Alfred, not very pleased. "Anyway, I *did*, and that is what matters. I decided I must have a fleet of ships, belonging to the country, and that these ships would be ships of war. I had them built specially for war on the Danes. The first ships I built were not as good as they should have been; but now they are improving, I hear from my messengers."

"And do your ships always beat the Danes?" asked Needler.

"Well. No, not yet," admitted Alfred, "But I think they will as soon as I have a few more of them. Only now the trouble is not only at sea. You see, lads, there have been a few kings before me who found an easy way out of war with the Danes by giving the Danes land, generally in the north of England. But that means that I have to guard against not only the Danes who come over the sea, but also those who are already

143

settled on the land. So I have organized two armies, who take it in turns to beat back the attacks of the Danes, both those who come in their ships and those who come from the north of England."

"Yes, that's all very well," said Jack Morris, "but what's the use of the fighting and working the way you do, when, as soon as you are dead and another king rules, everything goes wrong again, and the Danes are allowed to come and settle in the country, and so on?"

"Ah, but that will never happen," said Alfred; "now that I have got things going, England will never be beaten by the Danes again."

"Don't you believe it," said Mr. Rocket. Opening his eyes for the third time. "England will be defeated by the Danes, and a Danish king will rule the country which you are fighting for now. His name will be Canute."

"Never," said Alfred; "never!"

"Now, there you are," said Leonard Jackson, "you see, all the good things you do aren't much use really, and the bad things you don't do would at least be interesting to read about in history books. Richard had a hump and he killed people, and John told lies and oppressed the poor and killed Arthur, and Canute sat on his throne on the beach and defied the waves, and Henry the Eighth had hundreds of wives, and Richard had a lion's heart—I mean the real Richard, not the hump-backed one, and—"

"Who are all these people you are talking about?" asked Alfred. "I don't seem to know any of them."

"They are kings," said John Berry, "and they all did something queer or brave or bad or funny— anyway, they did something unexpected; but you, you don't seem to do anything except what you ought to do."

"This is too much," said Alfred, rising to his feet in annoyance. "You boys have no manners. Do you realize you are speaking to a king, and a very good king at that? You say I never do anything exciting. What about going round the country in disguise, as I am doing right now, pretending to be a minstrel, and going right into the camps of the Danes to learn their secret plans, so that I can surprise them on the field of battle? How many of you would dare do that? Night after night I've sat by a Danish camp-fire, plucking this harp and singing my songs to them, and I've actually heard them saying what they would do to Alfred the King of England if they could catch him. I've drunk wine with all the leaders of the Danes, and made up songs about their victories, and the very next day I've defeated them in battle because of the plans I've overheard. How many of you would dare to go into the enemy's camp and risk your lives in order to defeat him?"

"Well, that's quite good and clever," admitted Alan Hope, "we're not saying you're not brave. The only thing we boys think is that you are too good. You never seem to like doing any of the things boys like. In history we never read about Alfred the Great doing anything wrong. You see, you like learning to read, and you like reading learned books, and you like going to church, and you like writing and doing sums and going to school and all sorts of dull things, and you never do anything wrong. You're like George Washington, who never told a lie—at least that's what he said, and I think *that's* a lie anyway."

"The thing is," said Jack Crossley, "that now we've met you we can see that you're a good sort of man, not an awful sissy. But if we'd never met you, and only read about you in history books, we shouldn't like you very much, because it always seems as though you're better than we are; and when people tell us about you, they seem to think we ought to be as good. If we don't like reading lessons, people say 'when Alfred the Great was a boy, he *loved* learning to read,' and—"

"Well, you know, I didn't always like learning," said Alfred, "and I wasn't always a good boy, and I have done things wrong. For instance, there was the matter of the cakes—"

"We know about the cakes," said Arthur Black, "that's the bit of history everybody knows."

"Ah, yes," said Alfred; "but do you know the true story?"

"I dunno," said Morris.

"I know it," said Leonard Jackson. "It was once when you were driven from Wessex by the Danes, and you were wandering around the country disguised as a turkey—"

"A *what*?"

"Turkey, wasn't it? Oh, no—a pheasant. Well I knew it was some sort of bird."

"I think he means peasant," said Mr. Rocket, opening his eyes again.

"All right; peasant," said Leonard Jackson. "Anyway—"

"Eeee, a woodpecker," said Edgar White, scrambling up a tree.

"I never did," said Alfred indignantly.

"Never did what?"

"Wandered among the pheasants disguised as a woodpecker—"

"He didn't say that you wandered—"

"He said that I wandered about Turkey disguised as a—"

"No, I didn't; I said that it was a woodpecker," said White from the tree.

"How could a turkey be disguised as a wood pecker?" asked Mr. Rocket, opening his eyes.

"You're getting me all mixed up," said Alfred. "That boy said I was driven from Turkey by the woodpeckers, and wandered about—"

"Well, it was the cakes you were going to tell us about," said Alan Hope.

"Wandered about Denmark disguised as a cake," went on Alfred desperately.

"It doesn't sound right to me," said Mr. Rocket, and went to sleep again.

"Anyway, let me tell the story," said Leonard Jackson. "Once you were driven from your country,

147

which is Wessex, and you wandered about disguised as a peasant. Well, you came to a hut of a swineherd named Denewulf—"

"What's a swineherd?" called out Edgar White from his perch in the tree.

"A pig-shepherd," said Jackson. "Well, Denewulf knew that the poor peasant was really the King of England, but he told no-one, not even his wife. So you stayed many days with Denewulf, planning war on the Danes. Now Denewulf's wife, not knowing you were the king, thought you were lazy, because you didn't do any of the housework, and yet you ate her food and lived in her house. So one day, when she was baking, she decided to make you useful, and said: 'Here, you, just keep an eye on these cakes while I'm outside, and turn them when they're ready, and if you let one of them burn, well, I wouldn't want to be you, because there's no more meals in this house.' So the king— that's you—looked at the cakes, and the woman left them in your care. But you were stringing your bow, and thinking so deeply about the Danes, and how to collect an army, and about the sorrows of your country, that you clean forgot the cakes and let them burn. Then the swineherd's wife came back, and saw the cakes burning, and you sitting by them and not doing a thing, and she scolded you, and called you an idle good-for-nothing, and chased you out of the house. But then her husband came back, and said, 'It's the king,' and the woman didn't dare say what she thought about you then."

"So that's how they tell the story, is it?" said Alfred. "Well, well."

"Why, isn't that the true story?" asked Billy Bartlett.

Alfred beckoned them nearer. "Don't say a word to anybody," he said. "If all the history books say that I burned the cakes because I was thinking about my country, well, that's all to the good. Now, if I tell you the truth about the cakes, will you promise not to tell anybody, and not to let it get into the history books?'

"Sure," said the boys.

"Well," said Alfred, "it was like this. I was in disguise, as you said, and I couldn't get on with the war against the Danes, because I'd lost my army—I don't mean they were killed, I mean they had all gone home. They do that sometimes, you know, and it's a terrible business getting them together again. They'll fight when they see the Danes in front of them, but once the Danes are out of sight, all the army lays down its arms and goes home to milk the cows. It's quite a problem. I tell you. Well, wandering about, I came to the hut of Denewulf. Now, I knew Denewulf slightly, and he knew me, so I said to him, 'Look here, Deney, old man, I want to stay with you a few days, or maybe a few weeks, till I get my army back together again.'

"He couldn't say no, of course—you can't say no to a king—so that was that. But the first day I was there, his wife brought me a plate of her homemade cakes. Now I like home-made cake as well as anybody, but not cakes like hers. Just look at that tooth, boys—I

149

broke it on one of her cakes the first day I was there. Terrible things they were. The outside was as hard as granite, and the inside, if you ever got to it, was like a bad egg. You can't imagine anything like her cakes. At first I thought it was a plot to poison me, but then I realized that she was really proud of them, and expected me to like them. Well, now I made my great mistake. I've always been too polite and good-natured. I should have said straight away that I couldn't eat the things, and that they were dreadful—but no, I couldn't hurt the good lady's feelings, and when she asked how I liked her cakes, I said I thought them very good. It was my own fault, I know. You can guess what happened. It was cakes, cakes, cakes, from morning till night after that. I had to eat her cakes for breakfast—after breaking this tooth, I always crushed the things on a stone with my battle-axe; then I had cake with my dinner, and more cakes at supper—they gave me nightmares every night. Well, I had toothache, I had indigestion, and I came out in spots. I tried putting the cakes quietly in my pocket, and later giving them to Denewulf's pigs, but two of the pigs died, so I had to stop that. One day I ran away from the hut, determined to give myself up to the Danes rather than stand it any longer; but I walked in a circle in the forest, and came back to the hut in the evening, to find a dish of cakes waiting for me. I grew desperate. What was I to do?

"Next day Denewulf's wife asked me to watch the cakes while she did the washing outside. I remember the day clearly. I sat there bending my bowstring, and the good lady set her cakes before the fire, one by one, a deadly row. Then out went her washing. Who could resist the opportunity? I waited till she was well away from the house, and then I leaned forward, and with the tip of my bow I gently edged the first cake into the fire. No sooner was this one nicely burning than I did the same with the second one, and so on down the line—they were all burning merrily. Then I stealthily pulled them back again to their real position, and left them there, smoking away, and as black as cinders. Then I got up and hid my bow, or put it in my bed—I forget—and then I came back to my seat and sat deep in thought. Well, you know what happened next. The wife came back, and there was trouble—really I was most upset about it, but it's no use crying over spilt milk, is it?"

Twang! Thud!

An arrow was shuddering in the tree above Alfred's head.

The boys ducked and dived for cover like lightning. Alfred dropped flat on the ground. Mr. Rocket woke from his slumbers and stood up; an arrow parted his hair, and he immediately lay down again.

"Alfred of England," said a voice, "yield yourself to us, or die."

Alfred said nothing, but wriggled farther behind a log.

From the trees stepped a tall Dane, bearing a bow and carrying an arrow ready at the string. He stood beneath a leafy bough, pointing his arrow directly at the king. "Yield or die," he said, drawing the bow. At the same time another Dane appeared behind the tree near which Alfred lay.

"I will not yield," said Alfred, popping his head up for a moment; "come and take me if you can."

"Very well," said the Dane, "if you will not yield, you must die." And he drew back his arrow as far as it would go. Alfred went flat on the ground again, while the boys all gasped in horror as they saw the Dane about to release the long shaft with its deadly barb; and then Edgar White dropped like a stone from the tree above the Dane's head, and wrapped his legs and arms round the Dane's neck. The arrow left the string with a mighty twang, and went clean through the Dane who stood behind King Alfred; the bowman dropped his bow and grabbed Edgar White.

There was a wild flurry of arms and legs and heads, a great deal of screaming and shouting, and all the boys had piled on the Dane. He went down with a great crash before them. He was still holding Edgar White, and had now got him by the throat and was trying to choke him; but all the other boys were tearing at him, biting and kicking and scratching, so that he did not stand much chance. It was not long before they had him fast, six of them holding each of his arms, and six each of his legs; and just as they were drawing a breath of relief, they saw Alfred draw his sword and spin round to face the wood behind them.

The wife came back and there was trouble

The boys, too, turned and saw that they were in deadly peril, for two Danes stood there, sword in hand, about to leap on them and cut them to pieces.

"Get back," cried Alan Hope to the King, and at the same moment all the boys leapt for safety, leaving their captive free on the ground. But Edgar White failed to escape—still held in the mighty Dane's grip, he saw the swords of the other two Danes sweep up in the air, heard them whistle as they sliced down at his head. Hardly knowing what he was saying, he shouted the name that suddenly flashed before his mind— "Merlin! Merlin!'

What happened was so quick and unexpected that hardly anybody knew just what it was. There was a sharp ringing click, and the sword of the nearest Dane flew out of his hand and went flashing hundreds of yards up into the air. At the same moment the Dane himself received a blow that felled him like an ox, and yet there was no-one to strike the blow. Nobody saw it but everybody heard it, and everybody saw the man fall flat on his back; while it seemed that two strong arms snatched Edgar White from the man's grasp, and swung him rapidly but gently back among the boys. But this was not all; indeed, the most remarkable part of all this was still to happen. While the Danes and the boys were still gasping with surprise, and while one Dane still had his sword raised to strike at the boys, the ground behind the boys opened, and they tumbled head over heels inside—into the classroom.

CHAPTER X
HOW THE GREATEST ADVENTURE BEGAN

And now we come to the adventure about which everybody knows something; the adventure which made the boys famous throughout the world. If this adventure had never happened, *the Magic Door* would never have been written. But after all that I must tell in these chapters there was no end to the letters from people who had seen something of the boys' exploit, and wanted to know all about them. Their photos were in all the papers; they were invited to supper with dukes and duchesses and two millionaires; they were asked to write accounts of their school days, which were sold at sixpence a copy on the railway station bookstalls; and Mr. Rocket could have made a fortune, if he had wanted, by allowing inquisitive Americans to see the boys at work in the classroom—one shilling a peep. In a word, the boys of Standard Three became *famous*. And it all began with Cecil Carter.

It was not long after the *Alfred the Great* adventure. The boys were longing for something exciting to happen; they didn't mind what, and of course, somebody suggested the Magic Door. They knocked, and the Winged Boy came and talked to them in the usual manner. And then Carter said—Mr. Rocket remembered his words long after, for they led to more gasps of horror and thrills and excitement and adventure and astonishment than anything on both sides of the Magic Door—"I'm tired of only going into ordinary history; I wish we could go somewhere more exciting."

The Winged Boy looked up in surprise: "Exciting? Isn't history exciting enough for you, then?"

Carter shrugged his shoulders. "Well it's exciting in a way, but I would like something different. Different altogether. I'm tired of men. After all; history's only men. I'd like to go further back, before there were any men. Can't you take us somewhere different, where nobody's ever been before?"

The Winged Boy shook his head. "That's just what I can't do. I can only open a door into a time when somebody has been through it before. That's one of the laws of the Magic Door."

"So we can't ever go anywhere where nobody's been before?"

"No."

"But look here," said Wilf Charter, "if Time is your father, I don't see why you shouldn't go anywhere you want. If my father was Time, I'm sure he'd let me go to whatever time I wanted to go to."

The Winged Boy looked doubtful. "Yes," he said. "I never said Time couldn't take you into parts of history where nobody's ever been before. Time can do anything like that. But I can't."

"You mean," said Jack Crossley, "that you can only obey the Law of the Door, and so you can only take us to where the Door has been open before; but Time, if we asked him, could take us anywhere he wanted?"

"Yes he could," said the Winged Boy, "but I don't think he'd want to take you anywhere. He hates being disturbed, and he is a terrible old fellow, though he is my father. I don't suppose he would do anything for you."

"Still, we could ask," said Jimmy Corner; "that wouldn't do any harm."

The Winged Boy looked still more gloomy. "I wouldn't ask if I were you," he said. "Be satisfied with the adventures you're having, don't go looking for new ones—they may not be as nice as you think. Besides, it isn't wise to disturb Time."

"Why, what can he do to us?" asked Black.

The Winged Boy admitted he did not know.

"Well, if you don't know, I don't see why you should be frightened," said Norman.

"Frightened?' said the Winged Boy, with an angry frown. "Who said I was frightened? I was just warning you, that's all. If you want to take the risk of disturbing Time and asking for more adventure, do so by all means. I shan't stop you. There's nothing for me to be frightened of—I was only thinking of what might happen to *you*."

"We're not frightened," said Jones. "We'll take the risk."

"All right," said the Winged Boy. "Don't blame me for anything that happens."

"How do we send a message to Time?" asked Leslie Rodd.

"You can't. I am the only one who can do that," said the Winged Boy.

"How?"

For answer, the Winged Boy turned to the Magic Door, which was closed. The knocker hung in its place, and the door gleamed with familiar green light. The Winged boy stretched up his hand and took hold of the knocker. As soon as he touched it, light blazed out as if it were a green lamp, and it shone so brightly that all the classroom was lit up with a vivid green glare. Then the Winged Boy raised the knocker and knocked with it. No sooner had he done so, than every bit of light went out; the Door stopped shining, and turned a dull black; the knocker looked as dead as a cinder.

All the boys stepped back from the door, which now looked horrible, cold, and cheerless, almost like the gate to a tomb. Even the Winged Boy looked oppressed and nervous, and he stood back a little way, fidgeting with his wings. Meanwhile the sky outside the classroom window clouded over, darker and darker, as if at the beginning of a terrible thunderstorm, and the windows shook from time to time, though there was no wind at all.

Ever darker grew the room, and the boys stood in tense silence, all of them by now wondering if it would not have been wiser to have taken the Winged Boy's advice, and not called upon Time. And now they became aware of something new. The room was not only growing darker; it was growing warmer. They were not long in finding out the reason. The dead black metal of the Magic Door was hot. Heat was pouring out from it as if from a radiator. Soon it was too uncomfortable to stand near it, and the boys moved silently away to the other side of the room. Ever hotter grew the door, till the boys could even smell burning as the heat scorched the wood of the black board. How much longer was this to go on? The room was like an oven. And then, with the suddenness of lightning, the Magic Door sprang open.

There was no light the other side of the door this time, nothing but pitch blackness; but with the opening of the door the heat had diminished, for a cold blast of air swept in from the darkness beyond. For two or three seconds the boys waited in silence, and then a figure emerged. It was a grey bent old man, with a pinched white face and a straggly beard. Over his shoulder he bore a great scythe, and in his left hand he clasped an hour-glass. He walked, or rather shuffled, slowly into the classroom, and the door closed itself behind him. But as he put his foot within the room on the floorboards of the school, the floor began to tremble, and even the walls quivered, with a mighty confused ringing in the air that swelled until it seemed as though the solid earth was rocking on its axis. It was the chiming of every clock in the world, paying homage to the master of all clocks. They were ringing and ringing. From the humble alarm clock on the dressing table in the bedroom, which rang as if it meant to burst itself, to the great church clock in its tower, even Big Ben himself in his nest high above London, every clock struck its hours and rang its bells. The steeples were shaking; the belfries chattered with the din. Even the little wrist-watches, which had no bells, caught their breath as they ticked on their owners' wrists and lost two minutes. And the school bells and the factory buzzers started, too, and the Greenwich pips on the wireless pipped as if to burst the loud-speaker, and the sirens on the tugs out in the rivers blew though no hand had touched them, and the gun at Norwich fired on its own and killed a bluebottle. Policemen ran madly about the streets, people who had just begun to work stopped, and people who had just stopped began again. "What can it be?" was the cry. In the farthest corners of the world cuckoo clocks shouted "Cuckoo!" though it was midnight in Timbuktu, people jumped out of bed and began to pull their boots on the wrong feet. Never was such a din, such a rattling, such a beating of bells, such a whirring of wheels and springs heard in the world as every clock saluted the old master, Time. It was heard in the mountain fastness of Tibet, where the missionaries thought it must be an earthquake. It was heard in the Amazon jungle, where the natives thought God was turning the world inside out like the peel of an orange. And in the classroom, where the boys stood watching the old man himself, the noise was truly frightening, and Mr. Rocket had to remember a book in the cupboard and try to find it again. Old Time said not a word, but stood in the classroom quietly turning his head from side to side, looking at the boys, and listening to all the bells which were ringing for him. The loudest of them all was the school bell itself, for it was nearest, and it rang so hard that it deafened half the boys in Standard Five (which was just under the bell), broke the window with its clamour, and finally split itself in two down the middle, so that the Education Committee had to get a new bell the following week. It was five minutes before the noise stopped, and even then there were one or two excitable clocks in different parts of the world which couldn't stop, but went on for days till they rang themselves to death. But at last the ringing in the classroom stopped, and Time spoke.

His voice was hollow and grating, and seemed to come from a long long distance. It was a very old voice, yet dry and level and clear.

"Who disturbs Time?" he asked.

The Winged Boy stepped forward without a word.

His wings hung drably from his shoulders, and he looked like a little boy who expects to be sent straight to bed. The boys felt sorry for him. Mr. Rocket popped up from the cupboard, having found the book he wanted, and watched.

"My son," said the old man, "what is it?"

The Winged Boy pointed to the boys. "They want you."

The old man turned and stared at the boys with his pale eyes. He said nothing, but as he looked at them each of them felt something very strange happening. It was as if the other boys were not quite solid. When you looked straight at them it was all right, but each boy felt that when he wasn't looking, the others melted and became not real, but like somebody else.

This was through Time looking at them. Sometimes the boys looked like grown men, sometimes like babies—sometimes they weren't there at all, and this gave you a rather nasty feeling of loneliness, because it seemed as though they were gone for good; but when you looked again, there they were as usual. And instead of Mr. Rocket, there was a strange, grey-haired old man kneeling by the cupboard; though when you looked hard at him, it was Mr. Rocket again.

Then Time spoke. "Well?" he said.

Everybody looked at Cecil Carter, for it was his idea. He stepped forward nervously. "We want to go further back into the Past," he said, "and have adventures before there were any men."

It was nearly a minute before Time answered. Then he said one word: "Why?"

Cecil Carter found it hard to explain. "I don't know. We want bigger things to happen. We want to know how things were in the very beginning. Our history adventures have only been going into another land, where the people dress differently, but we want to go to a time when things were *quite* different, where it's not at all like the world we live in."

Time looked at the boy for nearly a whole minute without saying a word, and then he spoke. "Even this world you live in, and this place you are standing on, is strange and wonderful if you could see it through the eyes of Time. This solid classroom was not here a hundred years ago, and will not be here a hundred years hence. And what is a mere hundred years? If you could only see this very spot, as I see it, you would be surprised. I will show you; then you will see that even a classroom is a wonderful thing, with a strange story behind it. You shall watch this room through the eyes of Time. First you shall see this spot thousands and thousands of years ago. Watch!"

He ceased speaking, and lifting the hand which carried the hour-glass, he turned the glass upside down. Then the boys caught their breath with surprise, for it seemed as though the walls and the floor of the classroom turned into a kind of glass. The planks of the floor were still there, but the boys could see through them, and the solid brick walls also were transparent.

And the wonderful thing was what the boys saw through the walls and the floor.

Water!

Nothing but water, wherever they looked.

Beneath the floor it lapped in sleepy waves, eddying and bubbling up through the planks; and when the boys looked out through the walls, there was water too. Water as far as you could see, not a sign of land; blue water, and the sun smiling down on a landless, shipless sea; water to the world's edge, as far as the eye could see. Yes, and more wonderful still, as the boys stared down through the floor beneath their feet into the clear blue depths, there swam past the very spot where Mr. Rocket's desk stood, and under the front row of desks on the room, the forms of great tropical fish—sharks with cold watchful eyes and many tentacled octopuses. And even as the boys watched, the scene was changing. The forms of hills and long out-lines of land were rising in the distance from the blue water; the water itself was fading, becoming misty like the things in a dream after you have wakened. Beneath their feet the boys, staring down, could see land rising to view from the depths, and the strange croaky voice of old Time was saying, with a kind of low chuckle:

> "There rolls the deep where grew the tree,
> O earth, what changes hast thou seen!
> There, where the long street roars, hath been
> The stillness of the central sea.

*The hills are shadows, and they flow
From form to form, and nothing stands;
They melt like mist, the solid lands,
Like clouds they shape themselves and go."*

Now there was nothing left of the sea at all. Bare hills stretched away on either side of the classroom, and these, even as Time said, were continually changing from shape to shape, melting in the mist. It was like a new and slower kind of sea, in which the ever-changing hills took the place of waves—a sea made of land. Then trees appeared, first one, then many, till the hills were clothed and hidden by them, and even the classroom was filled with the trunks and branches of the great forest; and everything grew and fell in less time than it takes to tell it; a tiny leaf shot up in the classroom, swelled till its trunk filled half the room, wavered and fell, and disappeared beneath the ground before you could draw breath. There were brief glimpses of animals—deer which sped across the room and vanished like ghosts before you could be sure you had seen them; once, even, Gordon Merrit saw the outline of a tiger, but he could not be certain before it was gone. And all the time the desks and the cupboard and the blackboard and the walls and the boys and Mr. Rocket were still there, and these things, trees and animals, grew and passed *through* the real things which were in the classroom, so that the boys themselves began to feel like ghosts. And soon they saw what seemed like ghosts indeed, for real people came into the room from nowhere, and were gone again before you could say a word to them. They did not seem to see the boys, or even know the classroom was there. There were two savages fighting, but before you had time to see which was winning they vanished, and in their place stood a little mud hut, beside which three very dirty children were rolling naked on the ground. They did not look up at all at the boys, although they were rolling right through Leslie Rodd's legs, and their hut was built through Edgar White's waist. Then the hut was gone as if it had never been, and across the floor of the classroom spread a lovely velvety carpet of green grass. On this, as the boys watched, rose a little grey stone cross, or rather a simple pillar of stone, with two arms sticking out rather like a cross, but shorter. This, too, vanished, and in its place came what looked like a small church, but it did not stay long enough for the boys to look at it closely, or to go inside, as they wanted to do. It fell, and more trees grew over its ruins. Then these vanished, and a castle wall appeared. For a second the wall was clean and white, then ivy covered it, and then it crumbled in ruins. There was grass and trees again for a little time, and then a tiny, lovely brick cottage with children playing in the garden; and in the very place where the cupboard stood, grew a golden laburnum tree which flowered for a second, and then drooped, just as the children, too, suddenly stood up as grown people, old people, and then quietly fell down into the ground again and vanished. This somehow made the boys feel wretchedly sad, particularly as just where the little house has stood a stream now flowed, with steep banks, and the boys had a glimpse of other boys clambering down the side and trying to catch tadpoles in the water. And then the stream vanished, too, and the boys realized that the walls and the floor of the room were growing thicker and darker, so that they could not see through them; and before they could speak, the classroom was round them again, as solid as ever. "So you see," said Time, "that even an ordinary classroom has a long and exciting story behind it, if you could only see it."

"But I don't understand what it all was," said Lowther.

Time looked at him for a minute, and then said: "You have just seen all that happened on this spot, where your classroom stands, in the last hundred thousand years or so."

"But the cottage and the little children," said Jack Crossley; "where are they?"

"They were here three hundred and fifty years ago. No-one now can see the place where the cottage stood, or the garden where the children played. It is all forgotten. They are gone as if they had never been. Now the school stands in their place, and soon it, too, will be forgotten."

"But all the things that once *were,* and now are gone forever—can you see them all?" asked Maurice Lane.

"I can see them all," agreed Time. "I am the master of the hours and the days and the centuries. The Past and the Future are always before my eyes."

"And I suppose nobody else can see these things unless you let them?" said Morris.

Time nodded. "But there are few indeed who even see me."

"How long have there been men on the earth?" asked Alan Hope.

Time scratched his head. "Men? Let me see—a very short time. A few thousand years or so—say twenty thousand years, perhaps."

"And was there anything alive before then?"

Time smiled. "Was there anything alive? I should just think there was. For hundreds of thousands of years before the coming of men there were living things on the earth."

"They wouldn't be very big things, I don't suppose," said Squeak Morley; "little things like mice and so on."

Time was smiling again. "What makes you think they would only be small things?" he asked.

"Well, there wouldn't be anything very important before men."

Time was a full minute before he replied. Then he said: "Before men, there were great and terrible creatures on earth. Like men they were proud of their strength, and they seemed big enough to live forever. They lived for many thousands of years, but at last they passed away from the face of the earth, and the earth has forgotten them. There is no stranger story than the story of the earth—the story that only Time can tell."

"That's where I want to go," said Carter excitedly.

"Where?" said Time.

"To the world you were talking about—the world of thousands and thousands of years ago."

"You shall go."

CHAPTER XI
THE LAND OF MONSTERS

There was something different even about the Magic Door, right from the first. The doorway was dark, not at all like the shining doorway the boys were used to; it was more like going into a black cavern, so that your heart beat faster as you went in. And then you didn't come out straight away on the other side; there seemed to be a kind of tunnel, blacker than the blackest night, hot and stuffy. When you put your hands out, you couldn't touch the boy in front of you, which was a little alarming, since you knew he was there, and could hear him walking along—but you couldn't touch him. Denis Smith stretched out his arms to touch Maurice Lane, who should have been just in front, but he found nothing but dark steamy air. Groping farther in the dark, his hands met what felt like a face—a damp, cold face, rather like that of a frog, only much bigger. Smith said "Ow!" and after that kept his hands to himself.

At last they came out on the other side, and as Jack Crossley came through, the Door vanished behind them, and they were in a new world. For two minutes the party stood in dead silence. You could have heard a pin drop. Then Alan Hope said one word.

"GOSH!"

They never dreamed of anything like it.

They were in a forest, but the forest was made up of giant ferns instead of trees. Bigger than oaks, the monstrous fronds arched up over the boys' heads and branched into millions of bright green plume-like leaves picked out against the brilliant blue sky beyond. Among them stood other trees, unlike any that the boys had seen—trees with cones on them like pine cones, but much bigger, and trees whose leaves overlapped each other like the scales of a fish. Flowers there were none at all, but everywhere was brilliant green, and every now and then the straight stem of a palm tree, with its great broad leaves dropping over at the top. Near John Berry stood an enormous yellow toadstool, bigger than a man, and there were others among the trees. "It's wonderful," said Carter.

"It's creepy," said Martin.

"Look out," said Mr. Rocket.

His warning was necessary. Down from the trees above Bartlett's head was crawling a large insect. A really large insect. It was a kind of coloured dragon-fly, and it was roughly three feet across its wings. Two great feelers were waving in front of its head, its bright jewelled eyes were sparkling in the sun, and its great

172

wings were twitching. When Bartlett saw it directly above his head he gave a wild shriek of fear, and jumped six feet, flat on Alan Hope's toes—but nobody bothered about that. They were all watching the great insect, fascinated. Suddenly it zoomed up from the tree into the air, with a hum like an aeroplane, and bore down on Mr. Rocket. "Oh, keep it off, *keep it off!*" screamed Mr. Rocket, diving behind Jack Crossley. Edgar White seized a fern branch which lay on the ground, and smote at the thing with all his force. He missed, and the thing settled on Mr. Rocket, on his shoulders, its great waving feelers touching all over his head and face. Then Edgar White struck again, and this time he did not miss. He killed the insect and nearly killed Mr. Rocket. He hit him on the head as if with a sledge-hammer. The branch crushed the insect, with a horrible crunching sound, and Mr. Rocket fell to the ground unconscious.

"You've killed Mr. Rocket," said Edgar Grey.

"Well, if I hadn't, the dragon-fly would," said Edgar White. "I bet Mr. Rocket would rather have been killed by me than by a dragon-fly."

"I'm not dead," said Mr. Rocket, sitting up and rubbing his head, "I'm only laid out. If it hadn't been for my nerves of steel I probably would have been dead."

"He saved your life," said the boys, pointing to Edgar White.

"I'm very grateful to him," said Mr. Rocket, rubbing his head, on which a bruise as big as an egg was rising.

"Don't mention it," said Edgar White with a smile. "I shall always be glad to do the same for you again."

"Er—no, don't do it again." Said Mr. Rocket, rubbing his head; then suddenly he leapt up from the ground.

"Oh, what is it, what is it?" he yelled, snatching his hand out of his pocket, into which he had just been putting it.

The boys looked. Two reddish coloured claws were wriggling out of the pocket. Mr. Rocket tore off his coat and flung it away from him, and the boys crowded round to watch as it lay on the ground. Out of the pocket came a many jointed leg, and then another, and then a round shiny head with evil eyes and a couple of feelers, and then finally there crawled out on to the ground what looked like a very large red earwig, as big as a lobster.

"It's a scorpion," said Mr. Rocket. "It's a giant scorpion. I might have been poisoned. Perhaps I am poisoned. Perhaps it bit me. Do I look poisoned, boys? Tell me the truth, do I look poisoned?"

The boys were too busy killing the scorpion to answer, so Mr. Rocket felt his own pulse, and decided he wasn't poisoned. Meanwhile Black had got the venomous creature held in a forked stick, while the other boys stamped on it, taking care to keep their legs and ankles away from its fangs. Soon they had squashed it, and they felt a little safer. But these two insects, coming so soon after each other, warned the boys that they must keep their eyes wide open in this strange forest; for there were evidently some queer things about—just *what* things they were soon to learn in more detail.

When they had time to breathe, and Mr. Rocket had stopped feeling his own pulse to see if he was dying, they noticed for the first time that the forest was not silent. In the distance they could hear croaking noises, rather like the cawing of rooks, but louder and much harsher.

"What's that?" asked Borden.

"Popeye," said Alan Hope.

But it wasn't Popeye, as they found out later.

"Hoi, look at this beetle," said Corner in some surprise; and he might well be surprised, for the beetle was a foot long.

While the boys were watching the beetle, their eyes being on the ground, they did not notice the grey form which passed over them in the sky. Though they did not see it, it saw them, and wheeled twice in the sky above them before sailing silently away on its vast grey wings.

When they had watched the enormous beetle wriggle its way under the roots of a fern, the boys and Mr. Rocket decided it was time to do something.

"Now we're in this queer place, I vote we go somewhere," said Bobby McManus. "Carter should lead the way, because he had the idea to come here."

"Right-o!" said Carter. "Follow me, we're sure to get somewhere."

"I'm hungry," said Leslie Rodd.

"Well, if it's food you want," said Mr. Rocket, "just leave it to me. I'll get you your dinners. I've brought my gun, so I'll be able to shoot some big game."

As a matter of fact, it so happened that he did meet some big game later, but he didn't know how big it was going to be till he saw it.

"Can you shoot?" cried all the boys.

"Can I shoot!" echoed Mr. Rocket scornfully. "Can I shoot! Just watch this!"

He took his gun from his back, pointed it at a tree fifty yards away, and fired. The tree did not move, but Black's cap flew off.

"Wow!" shouted Black. "Who are you trying to kill?"

"Oh, I'm sorry," said Mr. Rocket. "I hadn't got my aim quite right. Let me try again."

This time the bullet sang past James Lock and nicked off the lobe of his ear, and after that the boys took the gun from Mr. Rocket. They said he was too dangerous. Alan Hope carried it, because he said he could shoot better than that with his eyes shut and both hands tied behind his back.

They hadn't gone far, Carter leading the way, when a strange creature like a cross between a kangaroo and a lizard came hopping out of the trees, it was a little taller than a man, and had some nasty teeth showing in its mouth. It saw the boys, but seemed afraid of them, and turned and hopped away, when Alan Hope put the gun up to his shoulder and sent a bullet into the animal's brain, a lovely shot which took it right under the left ear. The creature fell down, its legs kicking convulsively, and the boys ran up and, on Hope's instructions, began to cut it up ready for cooking. They would have cut it all wrong, however, if it had not been for Mr. Rocket, who told them which parts would do to cook and which parts should be thrown away. Some of the boys had already got a fire going, and as soon as possible the steaks of meat cut from the animal were hung over the flames. The boys sat around smelling the appetizing smell of roast meat. It smelt like beef; the boys were by now so hungry that they could hardly give it time to cook properly. However, it was quite tender and tasted like roast chicken.

Meanwhile, the boys had not neglected to keep a watch while they were eating; they didn't want anything to steal upon them unawares. Glover and Rodd were detailed to keep watch while the others were cooking and eating, and, to do them justice, they did not grumble at having to wait for their food, though they were very hungry; and the others saved the best bits of meat for them. Then, while Glover and Rodd came to eat, the others took their turn at watching, and also began to gather sticks, branches, and thick leaves of palm trees to make a hut in which to camp. Mr. Rocket was very useful at this work. Sitting on a pile of branches in the middle of the clearing, he told everybody just what to do, what branches to bring and where to stack them—in fact, he directed everything. It was only jealousy when Alan Hope said he ought to do a bit of work himself instead of telling other people what to do. Anyhow, Alan Hope didn't do much.

It was growing dusk when the hut was finished. There was plenty of room inside for everybody if they lay close together, and a nice raised couch for Mr. Rocket; only, by some mistake John Berry and Alan Hope were allowed to get on it, and they refused to get off, so that Mr. Rocket had to sleep on the floor.

Some of the boys wanted to explore the jungle a little further before going to bed for the night, but the others said it was too dangerous to wander among the ferns at night, for you never knew what you were going to run into; so in the end it was decided that nobody should leave the camp before morning. A fire was kept burning all night in case wild beasts or anything else came creeping up, and six boys at a time were to keep watch and tend the fire. Leonard Jackson was the captain of the first watch, and the boys under his command were Jones, Taylor, Martin, McManus, and Baker. The others all turned in and went to sleep—all except Mr. Rocket, who could not sleep because Hope and Berry had pinched his bed and White kept pushing his foot in his eye—Mr. Rocket's eye. But as it turned out nobody had much sleep that night.

About half an hour after darkness had fallen, Leonard Jackson's voice said; "Wake up, lads, there's something happening."

They awoke and listened with thumping hearts. There *was* something happening. It sounded as though an earthquake was happening. Something was crashing through the ferns and undergrowth near the camp— something which, from the sound it made, could not be much smaller than a tank, and might be much larger. Crump, crump, crump, went the mighty footsteps, ever nearer the camp, and the earth trembled beneath the enormous weight.

It was no use pretending not to be worried. Nobody on earth could hear a noise like that without feeling sick. It was a colossal noise, far beyond that an elephant would have made. Some beast, terribly larger than any the boys had ever dreamed of, was approaching the camp; the great ferns were crashing under its feet.

"It mustn't come any nearer," said John Berry, "it will crush us under its feet."

"Who's going to stop it?" said Mr. Rocket.

John Berry leapt up and ran out of the hut. "Stop!" cried everybody, for no-one wanted to go out and face what was there. The boys who had been on guard had crept shivering into the hut, and Berry was out alone.

"I'm coming," said Wilfred Charter, and followed Berry; and at this Mr. Rocket seized his gun and went out as well.

It was a fairly light night, with a bright moon, but there was a misty haze which made everything seem vague. Mr. Rocket stopped on the threshold of the hut, for he saw the two boys outside were looking at something. He looked, too, without saying anything, but at first all he could see was a tall tree near the hut. Then a queer chilly feeling got him at the heart as he suddenly realized that that tree had not been there when they built the hut. It was bigger than the other trees; it looked in the half-light rather like a lighthouse. And as the boys and Mr. Rocket watched it, it moved.

Brave as he was, when that great neck and evil snake like head came down towards him from the misty sky, John Berry fainted. A feeling of coldness swept over him, the night seemed to darken, and he slid to the ground. He was prepared for most things, but he had never dreamed of anything like that. Mr. Rocket could now make out the great bulk of the creature, stretching away among the trees; he could even see the moon gleaming on its tail, fifty feet long, and its massive legs, each bigger than a tree. Its eyes were cold and flat like the eyes of a fish, its mouth seemed wide and grinning, and its long neck curved down as it nosed the prostrate form of John Berry.

"Quick! The fire!" shouted Mr. Rocket, and at the same moment he put his gun to his shoulder.

Charter leapt to the fire and gave it a great kick. The flames and sparks shot twenty feet in the air as the dry wood caught again, and the whole scene was vividly illuminated. Mr. Rocket fired and missed completely, but it did not matter—the fire had saved John Berry. The head of the monster had only been a yard from the unconscious boy when the sudden blaze flared up. The creature started like a nervous horse; its head swept back on its long neck, and in a second the boys could hear it blundering and trampling among the trees as it turned and fled from something it had never seen before. Even then it came near to wrecking the hut, for, as it turned, its tail swept round and demolished a tree standing by the entrance. However, John Berry was safe; Charter dragged him into the hut again, assisted by Mr. Rocket, and he soon recovered from his faint. The rest of the night was less disturbed, but after this experience it was not easy for anybody to go to sleep, and in fact, most of the boys remained awake all the night. Mr. Rocket slept, partly because he had nerves of steel, but more because he knew the boys could not go to sleep, and they would wake him if anything went wrong. "And after all," he said, "why should I stay awake if they are doing so?" The fire was kept going full strength all the night, as high as the boys could pile it, for they didn't want any more visitors, and, as a result, everybody was roasted in the hut, or almost so. It was so hot they had to take off all their clothes; and because there was not much room in the hut and they were all piled on top of each other, when they put their clothes on the next morning they mostly got the wrong clothes, and they all turned out in each others' coats and trousers. Little Denis Glover was lost in David Rogers's navy suit, while Billy

Bartlett had one of Merit's boots on, and one of Bobby McManus's.

They stood outside the hut as the grey light of morning was breaking, gazing into the forest and wondering what surprises it held for them. Suddenly Squeak Morley gripped Jack Crossley's arm.

"What's that?"

"What's what?'

"There, in the tree—that grey thing."

"Grey thing—in the tree? There isn't any— Goodness! So there is! What a horrible thing. Whatever is it?"

In amongst the fronds of the nearest fern tree, sitting brooding over the camp, was the most ghastly thing the boys had ever thought of. It was the sort of thing you see in a nightmare. It looked like a grey old woman, crouched on a branch, with a dirty leathery cloak folded over her shoulders and over her head, and little sunken eyes, and a nasty vulture-like mouth. It was just like a dreadful old woman, and yet it was the wrong colour; half hidden among the branches, it seemed to be all grey, and there was no hair on its head—only dry grey skin like dirty leather. It was watching the boys.

At that moment Mr. Rocket came out of the hut. While all the boys were rubbing their eyes with tiredness, he was fresh as a daisy, for he had slept all night.

"Now," he said briskly, "what's the programme this morning?"

"Ssh!" said Jack Crossley. "Look!"

Mr. Rocket looked, but he had slept so well that his eyes were not working properly yet. "What have I got to look for?" he asked. "Only an ordinary fern tree, so far as I can see."

Jack Crossley put his finger to his lips. "Ssh! There in the shadows. Look!"

"Shadows my foot! Nothing there. You must be seeing things. Look, I'll go and show you—"

"Stop," hissed all the boys; but Mr. Rocket had strolled right up to the tree, and with two lively springs was up the trunk and among the foliage. Then he gave a dreadful scream of terror. He had looked up, and straight above him, a few feet away, he had found a face looking down. But what a face. It haunted him in nightmares years after.

He fell like a stone to the ground; his muscles would not support him; and then the grey creature moved.

It unfurled its grey cloak, and dropped like a stone on to Mr. Rocket. This would have been the end of Mr. Rocket if it had not been for the boys. Nothing could have saved him but the courage of Standard Three.

"Forward, lads!" shouted Hope, and they flung themselves towards the dreadful thing which sat on the chest of their teacher.

Then they saw what the cloak was. The creature sailed up from its prey on the wide wings of an immense bat. It was a bat; or, at any rate, something very like a bat, with wings twenty feet across. It sailed

183

over the boys like an aeroplane, snatching at them and trying to tear them with its cruel teeth; but they shouted at it and beat it with sticks, and soon it soared away, screaming harshly as it did so, with the very sound the boys had heard the previous day, and had ascribed to Popeye.

Mr. Rocket had come round from his swoon. "Good heavens," he said. "Keep it away."

"It's gone now," said Edgar White.

"What in the name of goodness was it?" asked Mr. Rocket.

"A pterodactyl," said John Martin, who had once seen a picture of such a creature in a scientific book. "It's a kind of reptile with wings."

"It's nasty," declared Mr. Rocket with conviction, and hobbled shuddering to the hut.

There was some meat left over from the previous night, so they had that for breakfast. It was all they had. It still tasted all right, but the flesh must have been different from the meat the boys were used to, since most of them felt rather sick after breakfast. This soon passed off, however, and they were ready to penetrate farther into the jungle.

The best way to proceed in the thick undergrowth would have been single file, but in this strange forest nobody was keen to lead the way alone, so the boys went two by two, with Mr. Rocket in the middle of the column. "In case," as he said, "any of the boys should need him."

You couldn't go far without something happening. Not fifteen minutes after they had set off there was a wallowing sound ahead. Everybody paused, and then crept on cautiously. Hope—as usual—was ahead. He pushed a trailing curtain of creepers gently to one side, and found himself gazing on a still lagoon, whose waters were blue in the far distance, but close at hand were muddy and overgrown with flat broad leaves. Hanging trees bordered the calm lake; the shore shelved gradually from shallow to deep; and there was a creature in the water.

This was the first full daylight view the boys had had of an inhabitant of the jungle of millions of years ago. It took their breath.

The nearest part of the creature to the boys was its head. This in itself was not so big—a little larger than that of a horse, perhaps, but all of it mouth. Then came a neck; it was not three feet long, nor six feet, nor yet ten. It was all of fifty feet—fifty feet of solid neck, growing thicker and thicker as it went further back towards the body. And the body itself rose clear out of the lake as big as an island—a monstrous hump of flesh; twenty feet of it were in view above the water, and the boys could only guess at the size of what was underneath the surface. But they didn't have to be content with guessing. As if to satisfy their curiosity, from the opposite bank of a small bay in the lagoon across which they were looking poked the head of another similar creature to the one in the water. As John Berry said, it was its wife—or perhaps its husband; at any rate, the new-comer was of the same type as the one in the water, and evidently knew it, for the two creatures made thunderous mooing noises at each other. The one in the water waved its head from side to side to welcome the one on the bank, while the one on the bank mooed and slithered forward through the trees towards the water. Now the boys could see it quite plainly. Martin, of course, had a go at naming it, and he said it was a diplodocus; then he said no, it wasn't, it was a plesiosaur; no, it couldn't be that, it must be a brontosaurus. Whatever it was, said Mr. Rocket, he wouldn't like to take it out on a lead. It sploshed into the water and waded like a moving island towards the other one, its mate, mooing happily all the time. Waves spread from its mighty legs and washed up on the bank where the boys watched this amazing sight. But there was more to come. While the boys were watching in awe and saying, "Ee, what a brimer!" a sudden crashing was heard from farther back among the trees not far off.

"Look out," said Baker; "something coming our way." The boys flung themselves under the roots of the nearest big plants, hoping not to find any giant beetles there, but naturally feeling that a giant beetle would be better than whatever was clumping and bouncing towards them. Nearer and nearer came the unearthly noise and thumping. It was quite as loud as the thing which had disturbed them the previous night. Then they caught a glimpse of it through the branches, and thanked heaven they had had sense enough to take cover.

It was an animal rather higher than a house, with the grey scaly skin of a lizard. It went forward on its hind legs, like a kangaroo, but waddling instead of jumping, and moving very fast. Its front legs were quite short, and ended in lizard-like claws, with which it grasped the trees as it moved along. Its mouth was terrible. It had no lips, but a long straight gash of a mouth, in which the teeth could all be seen; an immense mouth, big enough to bite a horse in two, or swallow a boy. Its eyes stood out sideways from its head, like great glass balls. It was so busy tearing its way through the wood that it did not see the boys, and for this they were very thankful. Lock whispered to Lowther: "Perhaps it doesn't eat flesh, perhaps it only lives on leaves and grass and stuff." Lowther had one look at the teeth in the monster's mouth and he knew what *he* thought about that.

The creature was in a hurry; it crashed past within ten feet of Bobby McManus, broke through the high ferns, and plunged down into the shallow water. At once the two reptiles already in the water mooed loudly with fear, and floundered away as fast as they could. The new animal was about half as big as they were, but the boys could see the difference clearly enough; the big creatures were as slow moving as oxen, and the other was as rapid as a tiger. Spurred by the sight of his prey, the new creature—which John Martin said was an allosaur, or a tyrannosaur—now bounded across the water in great spasmodic leaps, sending mud and water and weeds flying in all directions. The other reptiles blundered madly away—scrambling, splashing, and falling, writhing in the foamy water—but the allosaur sped towards them with its wicked eyes burning in its head and its dreadful mouth agape. One great reptile gained the shore, but here it was even more helpless than before; its legs could hardly support its great bulk out of the water. The other made one last despairing attempt to avoid its fearful hunter, slipped into the water and fell. At the same moment the allosaur leapt on it, and the boys saw those rows of murderous teeth sink into the thick part of the great creature's neck. It shrieked in agony, a blood-chilling sound that echoed over the still surface of the lake, and then there was the sickening sound of tearing flesh. With one bite the allosaur had almost severed the head of its victim; lifting to the sky its jaws all running with blood, it gave a wild and fearful cry of triumph. At that sound, the boys shuddered and put their hands over their ears. They could endure the sight of the monster tearing and rending his prey, but not the sound of that shocking cry.

Not content with killing one of the reptiles, the allosaur turned in, pursuit of the other. This great animal was endeavouring to escape among the trees, but hardly had it vanished before the allosaur was at the same place, making its way up the bank. And now the boys were to see an even more horrible thing than the slaughter of the first dinosaur. From the trees, flying silently but swiftly to the lake, came hundreds of pterodactyls, the giant bat-like creatures that had so scared Mr. Rocket. Like carrion crows they bore down on the still writhing corpse of the monster half-submerged at the edge of the lake. Their hoarse cawing was horrible to hear, far louder and far more wicked than the sound of crows. For a brief while they circled above the dinosaur, making sure it was no longer able to harm them; then with one accord they fell on its heaving sides, and the air was filled with the gruesome noise of their feeding. The boys looked and shuddered, realizing what would be their fate if the pterodactyls, rising from their horrid feast, should chance to see them. Hope turned to tell the other boys to retreat while they had a chance, but his words were cut short by a terrible sound from across the lake—the killing-cry of the allosaur. The other dinosaur had met its fate.

"I'm going," said Hope with decision; "anybody who wants to can stay by this lake, but I'm going, and I hope I'm not coming back."

"Lead on, Hope," said the boys, "we're going as well. We've had enough."

They turned like one boy and hurried away, following Alan Hope, anywhere away from the shores of the dreadful lake. Before them the mighty ferns raised their proud plumes, the palms spread out against the sky, and in the background was the darker green of the conifers; pale toadstools and other fungi gleamed amid the stems of the plants, and ugly insect forms, far larger than any insects ought to be, moved to and fro in the shadows. On the boys plunged, horrified by what they had seen at the lake, and thinking only of getting as far away as possible. This haste nearly cost them their lives.

Diving round a clump of ferns, the boys broke into a clear patch of land in the midst of the jungle—and fell back in terror from the form which was waiting there, as if it had heard them.

Its snout was no more than a yard away from the foremost boy, Alan Hope, and in the shock of seeing it he fell headlong on the ground, he didn't stay there long. The creature walked forward and *prodded him with its nose.*

Hope leapt like a jumping-cracker to join the other boys, who were in full retreat. John Martin alone stood for a second to look with round wondering eyes at the animal approaching. "It's a stegosaur," he cried, but nobody wanted to know. They just wanted to go a long way in a short time.

There is no way to describe a stegosaur. I could say that it had a mouth like that of a rhinoceros, eyes like a pig, and a fringe of spikes all down its back, and that it was as tall as four elephants. But that wouldn't give you any real idea of the thing. You will have to look at the picture facing page 200 to understand just why Alan Hope, who was no coward, suddenly began to travel faster than he had ever moved in his life. And even when you see the picture, you can't have any idea of how the creature sounded as it crashed and lumbered on the boys' heels, like a tank going through the primeval jungle. "Run, run, *run!*" howled the boys at the back, pushing frantically at the others in front of them, scrambling over one another's feet in their desperate endeavour to get away. And ever nearer came the monstrous crashing, and the flying schoolboys cast terrified glances over their shoulders and ran on, panting and white-faced. But to escape the four-footed giant was hopeless; the stout ferns, the rushes and canes which held the boys back were brushed like straws from the shoulders of the beast, and in a minute or two its breath would be on their necks. It was the end. With a weak pitiful cry, Hope, who was still last of the flying boys, threw up his arms and dropped in the path of the onrushing monster. The other boys heard him and turned; they could not save him—that they knew well—but they could die with him. In that terrible moment not one of the boys would have deserted the gallant ginger-haired lad who lay prone before the stegosaur. Only Mr. Rocket, supported by his nerves of steel, fled on, but looking once too often behind him, ran headlong into a tree, and dropped unconscious.

Hope lay there just as he had fallen, one hand flung out before him, his face buried in the rank grass. It seemed a matter of seconds only before those terrible paws would crush him to a red pulp. Nearer, nearer— the evil pig-like eyes, the senseless gaping mouth, and the pounding paws, each one thumping the ground like a steam-hammer. And then the monster stopped; over the horrified cries of the boys, over the hissing breath of the stegosaur, came a different sound, a louder sound—a fearful high shriek—half-laugh, half-roar—the hunting cry of the allosaur. The boys saw it, even as the stegosaur halted and twisted its head aside. There it came, the allosaur—there, over the waving ferns and the canes, leaping with mad ferocity, its wide lipless jaws displaying those dreadful teeth, one snap of which would have cut a horse in two. Bigger than a house and faster than a whirlwind, it fell on the stegosaur, dropped down on its back, and with one bite had torn out all the side of the creature's neck. It was a sickening sight; the boys were not a dozen yards away from it. Hope crawled forward, trembling in every limb; and Mr. Rocket, who had just sat up and was rubbing his head, turned even paler and crept behind the tree he had run into.

And he did right. The allosaur was not killing for its dinner. In the two dinosaurs it had killed earlier it had enough meat to feed it for days. It was killing for the joy of killing, and nothing that moved was safe from the allosaur at that moment.

The boys were crawling away, keeping down in the long grass, and perhaps if each boy could have done this, all would have been well. But Mr. Rocket was not in good cover behind his tree, and it was certain that as soon as the allosaur had finished with the stegosaur it would see him; and to make matters worse, he had given himself such a terrific knock on the head that no sooner was he behind the tree than he fainted again. To leave him could only have meant one thing—he would have made one mouthful to the allosaur. For all his misdeeds, the boys could not leave their teacher to this terrible fate. Edgar White and Jack Crossley seized a foot each, and John Berry and Baker a hand each, and they tried to pull their teacher to safety.

They would have succeeded, if only Mr. Rocket had remained unconscious; but as they pulled him, he half woke, and shouted out: "Hoi, who do you think you're pulling?"

That did it. The sound of tearing flesh, which indicated that the allosaur was still busy with the stegosaur, ceased immediately, and the creature reared its head to find where the sound came from. First to one side then to the another it looked, while the boys trembled and dared not breathe; and then Mr. Rocket, still half-conscious, shouted: "Who's that pulling my leg?"

The allosaur saw them. Its glassy eyes fixed on them all as they crawled towards the cover of the trees. They saw its great hind legs tense for a forward lurch, and they all jumped to their feet in dread, to run for it. There was only one way to run—straight forward between two rocky walls. Forward they ran, dragging Mr. Rocket with them, and noticing, even in their terror, that the ground beneath them seemed strangely springy. There was no hope of escape. Over their heads sounded the high gurgling cry of the allosaur as it reared over them—and then they were falling, falling, falling into inky darkness.

CHAPTER XII
THE CAVE OF HORROR

Darkness and a rocky floor. The boys landed in a writhing heap, and, needless to say, Mr. Rocket was at the bottom. Over them crashed the footsteps of the baffled allosaur, while they had fallen through a rift in the earth, no more than two foot wide, extending for perhaps thirty feet between the rocky walls above. This crevasse had been masked by the thick rushes and trailing plants, so that none of the boys had seen it till too late; but they were not sorry to be saved in this way from the flesh eating creature above, even though it cost them a bruise or two. And, anyway, their fall was broken by Mr. Rocket.

They picked themselves up, rubbing elbows and knees, and began to explore. They were in a deep rocky cave, about fifteen feet below the level of the ground. They had not fallen straight down, or many of them would have been killed, but had slid down a very steep slope, which in the end precipitated them over a sheer drop of no more than a foot or two on to the rock floor.

The first thing the boys realized, and it was a serious thing, was that they could not get out of the cave the way they had come in. It would be like climbing on an almost sheer wall of smooth slippery rock. Unless there was another way out of the cave, they were in a fix.

It was minutes before their eyes became sufficiently used to the darkness to see about them. The cave was not pitch black; through the opening by which the boys had fallen came a glimmer of light. This revealed, after the boys had strained their eyes for some time, that the cave was not round, though it ended in a kind of circular wall where the boys had fallen. The other end retreated into the shadows—in fact there was no other end. Poking gingerly along into the darkness, White found a kind of continuation of the cave, an underground passage which seemed to lead upward.

"Look here, boys," he said, "the cave goes this way and I think it leads back to the surface again."

The other boys could not see quite so well.

"Right-o, you lead the way, Edgar," said Alan Hope, and the rest of them groped towards Edgar White. He was right about the cave. It did go in that direction, and once they had turned the corner in the rock, they found the passage was lit by a faint grey light which filtered through from the crevasse above. But here they had a less pleasant discovery. The passage no longer sloped upward to the ground, but began to descend pretty sharply. They had to follow it—there was no other way—and the tunnel sloped ever more steeply downward. As they went on, the boys noticed that the bluish rock walls of the cave were gleaming with moisture, while the air turned cold, wet, and stagnant. Soon all the boys were shivering with cold, and only the knowledge that they could not get out if they went back made them go on. Then came a corner, a turning, after which all was dark, for the fissure in the earth above had come to an end. Here five of the boys, who carried sticks from the ferny plants above, set their sticks alight with Mr. Rocket's matches, and thus made torches. Fortunately the wood burned very well, with a bright reddish light which lit up all the walls of the cavern. And now an amazing thing happened. The boys rounded a bend in the winding passage, and those who were at the back of the column let out a cry of surprise; for they could see two lots of boys in front of them instead of one, and the new lot of boys were walking upside-down, carrying their torches, underneath the feet of the real boys, about twenty feet down.

Everybody stopped to investigate this strange appearance, and it did not take long to realize that the new, upside-down boys were the reflections of the others. As Hope held out his torch, they could all see that now they were walking on a quite narrow ledge of rock, about ten feet above an underground lake. The lake stretched flat as a glass far into the shadows; the boys couldn't see where it went to. They didn't want to look, for they were far more interested in gazing straight down into the depths of the lake itself—and this was for a very good reason.

Above the heads of the party of schoolboys soared the splendid natural roof of the cavern, higher and ever higher, till it vanished in the shadows beyond the light of the torches. Wherever the flickering glare of the torches caught the roof, it glanced and danced with a million sparkling diamond-points of colour, for the roof was entirely hung and covered with curtains, shimmering draperies, of stone—shining stalactites. On these countless needles of brilliant stone the torchlight played like witchfire, and the glorious display was reflected, spark for spark, in the still waters below. No wonder the boys stood and gazed. Never had they dreamed of such a fairyland of light and colour. With every waver of the torch-flames the magic scene below them changed and varied, so that one moment it was a forest of decorated Christmas trees, and the next a magnificent cathedral, where the lights were like the setting sun through stained-glass windows.

Then, as they watched, without any warning the surface of the water moved. It lapped heavily against the rock wall; and for the hundredth time that day the cold hand of fear seemed to grasp the boys' hearts. For if this underground lake moved—this lake where no breeze could reach—there must be something to move it. And what could it be that stirred the waters five hundred feet under the earth?

They were answered.

Not thirty feet from them a head broke the surface of the water, and two great eyes stared at the boys. A mouth opened—a mouth bigger than the mouth of a hippopotamus; and then the head reared itself out of the water on a neck nearly four feet thick, and unbelievably long. And the whole of the head and neck—this was the horrible thing about it—were white, a dirty white, the colour of a creature which spent its life in darkness.

While the boys, spell-bound with horror, stared at the great head and neck which was rising from the water, the monster was not wasting time. Evidently the lake was shallow here, for the reptile reared up on stout legs and launched itself at the boys. And here a terrible accident happened. Spinning on his heel to run away, Harry Lowther slipped on the smooth rock and went over the edge.

Below, the water swelled and rippled darkly with the every movement of the reptile which was wading out.

Baker flung himself face down on the rocky shelf and caught Harry Lowther by the sleeve just as he slipped. Could he hold him? Lowther was no feather weight, and Baker's grip was not very firm—and the hungry water eddied ten feet down beneath them. The monster wallowed towards them; Meredith Jones dropped to help Baker. "Hold him a second longer," he cried. "I'll have a grip on him in a tick." He stretched out his arm; Lowther's sleeve was but an inch away from his hand when Baker said with a despairing gasp: "I can't hold him any longer"—and then, splash!

Lowther had fallen into the sullen lake.

This was the end, thought the boys. Nothing could escape the creature in the lake; it would swallow Lowther in one bite. But they were wrong. The great head of the reptile swayed to where Lowther had struck the water, and nosed down in search of him; but after a short time the head came up again, and the monster gave a long resounding roar of baffled rage. And no wonder. It was beaten by its own enormous size. Lowther had fallen into the shallow end of the lake, and getting to his feet immediately, had naturally backed away to the rock wall, as far as he could get from the reptile. But he could not find the rock wall; instead he banged his head on a projecting ledge above him, and soon realized that there was a deep recess under the wall, running all the length of the lake. Into this recess he backed, ducking his head, for the rocky roof above him was only three and a half feet from the floor; and he found he could get nine or ten feet away from the rock face. He was not long in scuttling right to the back, where he stood, up to his knees in water, and anxiously waited to see if the monster could get him. It could not. Its head was much too big to get under the recess roof, and its feet also were too thick to poke the boy out with. Hence the creature's rage; it

Never had they seen such a fairyland of light and colour

The monster stopped

knew there was something there which ought to be good to eat, but it couldn't get at it. And while it was poking about trying to get Harry Lowther, the boy was working his way along the cave towards the end of the lake. A strange thing now happened. While Harry Lowther, under the ceiling of rock, was moving to the right, towards the place where the high ledge from which he had fallen met the ground, the boys on the ledge were also moving the same way, for the simple reason that the infuriated reptile was chasing them. It sploshed through the water with its head on a level with the ledge, trying to lick the boys from the ledge into its dreadful mouth, but missing them all the time because they were running so fast. Naturally, at the point where the ledge above joined the ground below, the boys came down to the ground and Lowther came out into the open—for there the recess ended! So Lowther and the other boys met, and very startled they were, too, to meet in that way. However there was no time for handshakes; on they all raced together, Mr. Rocket urging them to ever greater efforts with his shouts of terror. Behind them pounded the monster, before them stretched the long darkening vastness of the cave—for they had missed their own path, which was narrow, and were now in an immense subterranean cavern. There could only be one outcome of the chase. In the cave, the monster's natural home, they could not possibly escape. Then came the end of the cave—a solid wall of rock, with not so much as a crevice for them to get through.

There was only one thing to be done, and it had to be done quickly; they could not go forward, for the rock barred their way; and they could hardly go backward, considering what was coming up behind them. "The Knocker!" shouted everybody, and they meant it.

No sooner said than done. Crossley had the knocker against the rock wall, and raised it to deliver the knock which would save them; but it was late, terribly late, to think of that. Like an avalanche the monster came down on them—it was there, on their heels, even as Crossley knocked—the rescue came too late.

Down, boys, down on your faces on the floor," shouted Mr. Rocket, who was already down—trust him! They flattened themselves on the stone beneath them as the monster rushed up, and then—well, it couldn't be helped. Anybody could see what was going to happen—nothing could have stopped it.

The Winged Boy had often told the boys that the door would grow to the size of anything which wanted to go through it—a big man could get through as easily as a boy. Now they had a chance to see this for themselves. There was no stopping the monster, with all the speed it had got up. It thundered on—the Magic Door sprang into view in the rocky wall—the door grew to the size of a church—and the monster thundered through.

CHAPTER XIII
HUNTING A MONSTER

You have read the newspaper accounts, and you won't want to be wearied by having all that stuff over again. It was the wonder of the whole world for half a year, and there are still pictures of all that happened on that memorable day to be seen in any museum. For this reason I will not give a detailed account of the appearance of the monster in the classroom of Standard Three at Chiltern Street Boys' School, but will simply put in this passage, taken from the Evening Telegraph and North of England Post, which is a statement by an eye-witness, a lady who saw the whole thing. "Interviewed by our reporter, Mrs. Mirtle, who is now in hospital recovering from the shock, gave a graphic description of the first appearance of the monster. 'I was outdoors, cleaning the parlour window,' said Mrs. Mirtle, 'and had just wrung out my wash-leather when I heard a tremendous crash in the school across the street, and a kind of tearing noise. At the same time the ground shook violently, and the window which I was cleaning cracked, so that my arm went through, and the glass cut me to the bone. But I was so frightened I didn't think of that, for I was sure it was an earthquake. I turned round to look at the school, and to my horror I saw all the roof of one end of the school lift sharply into the air, and then the walls and roof seemed to crumble into just loose bricks and mortar, and it all came thundering to the ground, and there, underneath what was left of the roof, sticking up through all the wreckage, was an enormous creature the like of which I never saw in all my born days, nor never want to see again. It was like a nightmare, this great thing, bigger than the school. By this time, of course, all the boys and teachers were rushing out of the school, and I didn't want to see any more, but I shouted out, "It's the end of the world," and I ran into the house and got under the table. Then I heard crashings and wallopings, but I didn't dare look out to see what was happening, and all the time the house was shaking fit to bust'"

And that was how it looked to the people on the other side of the Magic Door.

Meanwhile the boys had got to their feet, trembling at what might happen now the monster had gone through into the ordinary world. The Winged Boy stood at the door looking pale and anxious, and said: "For goodness' sake go after it and do something. Something terrible will happen now that thing has got loose!" The boys, forgetting their fear, ran through the Magic Door into what had been their classroom—but what a difference now. The desks and the floor were crumbled into matchwood, and all the end of the school where their classroom had been was a heap of rubble, with bricks and tiles still falling thunderously from the part of the school which was still standing. The belfry with the familiar school bell lay shattered in the ruins of the playground, and what had been the hall was a mere rubbish heap of wood and plaster. And worse was in store; for as the boys stood in shocked silence to see this destruction, to their ears came a sinister sound of crashing walls, and a loud continual screaming as frightened people ran from the path of the monster.

The boys rushed out into the street and saw a sight such as had never been seen before in the history of man. Down the whole length of the street the houses were lying in ruins, not only knocked down, but trodden flat; and in the distance the monster moved on—they could see it towering high above the houses—scattering rows of houses with its feet as if they had been made of cardboard. Only one attempt was made to check it; the soldiers at a near by barracks had fired on it, but their bullets had made no impression at all on the immense creature, and it had torn fearfully on, crushing everything in its way. There was a field gun at the barracks, which might have had some effect, but nobody had thought of it till the creature was a long way past, and even then the officer said he could not allow the gun to be fired without orders from the general.

The boys raced after the monster, not knowing what they could do, but determined to stop it if it could be stopped. They came to the barracks, and here they stopped with one accord.

They had all seen something at the same time. If this could not stop the creature, nothing could.

It was a tank.

It stood outside the barracks, ready for manœuvres in the field—an enormous new tank, the heaviest made, equipped with two shell-firing guns and several machine guns.

The officer stood there, white-faced, gazing after the monster which had passed. "Stop it, somebody stop it," he was moaning, but he didn't make any effort to stop it himself.

"Get after it with the tank, man," said Hope impatiently.

The officer looked at him in horror. "The tank?" he said. "Oh, no; I couldn't do that. The tank is only to be used when the general gives orders—"

"Don't be silly," snapped Mr. Rocket. "That thing there has to be stopped, and there's nothing but a tank will stop it. Get into the tank quick and go after it."

"Oh, no; I couldn't do that—"

"Quick, boys," rapped out Hope. "While we're talking, that thing is killing people. Get into the tank."

"Stop! Stop!" shouted the officer, but nobody took any notice of him. "Into the tank, boys," cried Berry, and in ten seconds they were all pouring in through the trap-door at the top. Mr. Rocket was last, and he got stuck in the trap-door, and had to be pulled through by his legs. He was always awkward.

Bartlett was at the controls before all the boys were well inside, and the tank leapt into life with a menacing roar. "Stop!" shouted the officer, dancing about outside, but Bartlett drove straight at him, and he dodged for his life. And then the chase was on.

Down the ruined street the tank rolled, gaining speed every minute, its caterpillar tracks clanking and whirring over the ground. Soon the boys had evidence that they were on the trail of the monster. The remains of a horse, torn in pieces, lay in the road in a sea of blood. A little farther on a tram had been kicked over, and lay on its side, with splintered glass all round. Shop-fronts were knocked in, lamp-posts and telegraph-poles strewed the ground, and in one place lay the body of a policeman. Other people there were none—they had fled, like rabbits, from the path of the monster.

The one fear of the boys was that the creature would turn to the centre of the city. So long as it kept on its present path, headed for the river and the docks, it would find few people to attack. But even as the boys thought of this, they gasped with dread, for straight before them, in the distance over the housetops, they could see the monster, and it was coming back towards them.

"Well, lads," said Hope grimly, "it's us or it. It mustn't get past us, or it will go straight back into the middle of the town. We must stop it now, or die."

Bartlett did not hesitate at the controls. Straight on he drove, through the walls that still remained of the houses which the monster had destroyed. Now they could see it clearly, straight in front of them, coming head-on for them. It was time. "Stop her, Billy. I'll have a go at it," said John Berry, who was at one of the guns. Bartlett did so; the tank grated to a stop. Berry stood like a rock gazing out over the sights, and then his hand fell on the gun controls.

"Crash!"

The gun spoke once, and the monster stopped dead. It was as if the great creature was trying to think. It looked strangely at the tank. What was this queer new animal, which was able to hurt it without coming near? It must look closer into this . . . At the same time a river of blood welled up in the reptile's shoulder and flowed down its foreleg.

The ravenous monster ambled nearer, looking beadily at the tank. Then John Berry went into action again.

Bang!

This time the monster definitely shook at the blow, for the shell ploughed a deep furrow in the flesh of its side before passing on to explode somewhere over the river. If either of Berry's shots had hit the reptile square in the chest that would very likely have finished it. However, after a brief pause, the boys saw that their aim was accomplished. The creature stood for a time, trying to think out this new situation. Then it wheeled lumbering round and headed straight away from the tank.

"Hurrah, Hurrah!" shouted the boys. "We've got it on the run!" And now they thought they had nothing to do but go in and destroy it. Bartlett, Hope, and Needler flung themselves at the controls of the tank; it pitched wildly forward, and in two seconds the boys were tearing in pursuit of the escaping monster. The motors, driven almost past their capacity, filled the tank with the din of their screaming, while the boys were thrown from side to side as the tank rocked over every obstacle. Nearer and nearer they drew to the massive creature which was fleeing from them; it could only be a matter of minutes now before they overhauled it, and Berry was already crouching over the gun, when suddenly Hope shouted "Stop! Stop! Stop! The edge!" and leapt to a brake handle.

The tank stopped with a heave and a jerk which nearly turned it over, and the boys picked themselves out of the front of the machine to see the reason for Hope's desperate action.

The tank was within ten feet of the edge of the dock; but for Hope's promptitude at this moment they would have been boxed up in the tank at the bottom of the river. The monster had beaten them; it had gone where they could not follow. While they poured out of the tank and lined up on the dockside, it had slipped straight down into the river, and even now was swimming out into midstream, while the wave of its going swelled and broke round the dock walls, shaking and battering the wooden piers.

"It'll drown," said Lock hopefully. "We needn't worry any more. Now it's gone into the water, that's the end of it."

"Drown, will it?" said Borden, and the others echoed him; "that thing can live in water as well as on the land. And what's it going to do to any ships it happens to meet, if we don't go after it and settle it? It's big enough to sink anything smaller than the Queen Mary."

"But we can't go after it. There's nothing to go in." Hope's eyes were fixed on something farther along the dock; one after the other the boys turned and followed his gaze, and as they did so, a light came into their eyes.

There, moored on the quay, was the submarine Winkle, which was paying a visit to different British ports. Nobody was on it except a watchman . . .

"Gerroff!" shouted the watchman "Gerroff! Run away! Be off! You can't come on."

"Rush him, lads," said Hope briefly.

They rushed him. He struggled wildly, but it wasn't long before he went over on to the quay, with a bump. Bartlett was already below in the engine-room; the plates of the submarine thrilled and quivered with the throbbing of the motors. The screw began to revolve. Looking out over the river, the boys saw a barge, half a mile out, overtaken by the monster. Faint cries of terror reached their ears; they saw one or two dark forms leap wildly off the deck to try and seek safety in the water. The barge was sucked under the creatures neck, the great mouth snapped down on a man on the deck, and the animal swept on; behind it the barge reappeared, upside down.

"See that?" said White. "That's what's going to happen to hundreds of ships unless we stop it."

Now the submarine was moving away from the quay; Barlett was in charge below, with Merrit, Black, McManus, Rogers, and Norman to assist him. Hope was the captain, and Berry the mate. Mr. Rocket made himself useful wherever he could. Soon the mouth of the river came into view, and then the boys were off on their eventful cruise. Evidently the news of their voyage and its purpose had already got abroad, for as the submarine, sailing on the surface and about a mile behind the hunted reptile, passed a destroyer at the river mouth, the destroyer fired its guns in salute—a salute which caused much alarm to Mr. Rocket, who thought they were being fired on.

After this hours passed without their sighting another ship. Fast as they were steaming the monster in front was out distancing them. From one mile it gradually increased its lead to three, and soon it was so far ahead that they could not see it without using a glass. Some instinct was guiding the creature south, down through the North Sea, and towards the English Channel. It turned into the Channel and passed only a mile out from the beach at Dover. Here hundreds and thousands of people thronged the beach, gazing out at sea with telescopes, and again the boys heard the thunder of guns fired in salute. Then came a fearful encounter. A tramp steamer was coming towards the Straights of Dover. Though it was not in the monster's path, the great creature turned aside and made straight for the ill-fated ship. The boys knew what was going to happen, and put on every ounce of speed, but they could not make the distance. The animal bore down on the ship; within about twenty yards, it suddenly threw itself bodily up out of the water, all the front part of its body being quite clear of the surface, and then dropped down on the tramp steamer. Not a man was saved.

After that, the boys could do nothing but hang desperately on to the trail. Out from the Channel by Land's End went the reptile, the boys still keeping it in sight; the whole frame of the submarine shook with the pounding of the engines. By now the boys began to think that this was going to be a long chase. The reptile seemed as if it could go on swimming forever; but fortunately the submarine's tanks were filled with oil, so that the boys could follow as far as the monster could lead. The sun was dropping to the western horizon, and the boys were already wondering how they could keep on the trail during the darkness, when they suddenly realized that this would not be necessary. Tired at last of its swim, and finding no land anywhere to rest its legs, the creature was turning back to the land it had left. First the boys saw the creature broadside on instead of only seeing the back of its neck, as they had before; then it turned fully round, and came straight back at the submarine.

"Say, look here, boys," said Captain Hope, "it's coming back. Now, everybody on the alert. It mustn't get away. This is our chance Jones and Morris man the torpedo tubes. Berry, take hold of this telegraph and signal whatever is necessary to Bartlett in the engine-room. I'm going forward. Dive her."

Berry dived. The conning tower and all the hatches were closed, the diving rudders set, Hope took his post at the periscope, and down went the submarine into the translucent green water, ten feet below the surface. Hope could see the head of the monster on the screen of the periscope. "Here she comes," he cried, and Jones shouted across to Morris. The moment had come. Jones pressed his button; silently the torpedo sped from the submerged vessel, away on its errand of death. At last the aim was true; the explosive cigar of steel took the reptile full in the chest, so near to the submarine that the explosion rocked the vessel and sent the boys sprawling on the floor. The force of the detonation nearly ripped the animal in two. It thrashed and beat in the water for a minute or so, turning all the waves red with its frothy blood; then its struggles ceased, and it floated to the surface, belly upward. The monster's brief excursion into the twentieth century was ended. There is little need to tell of the boys' triumphant return, and how they were saluted by squadron after squadron of battleships on their way back, and how the King sent for them to come to his palace in London and presented each of them with a purse of gold and a platinum medal, of how dukes, duchesses, and two millionaires—as already related—gave banquets in their honour, or how they became rich beyond their dreams simply by writing about their adventure in the Sunday papers. These things were common knowledge.

What is perhaps less well known is the subsequent career of that great teacher and splendid man, Mr. Rocket. Shaken to the core by the unparalleled horrors and perils through which he had passed, the lion-hearted schoolmaster could not bring himself to return to the classroom; his princely salary being thus at an end, this valiant gentleman contrived to eke out a small livelihood by selling the composition books of Standard Three to American millionaires—fifty pounds a book. The fortune he made in this way did not last long, however, since his needs were great. Within a year he had spent it all on ice-cream, fruit-machines, chewing–gum, swings, roundabouts, switchbacks, fairy-cycles, Meccano sets, motor-boats, Hornby trains, roller-skates, and more chewing-gum. Faced with poverty, Mr. Rocket had no alternative but to ask the Education Committee if they would take him back. They did; Mr. Rocket went back to the old school. When he went into the classroom, Standard Three were waiting for him; they sang:

"Good-morning, dear teacher; good morning to you."

We have reached the end of our story. Jack Crossley still has the knocker, Mr. Rocket is at the end of his money, and the class still awaits the next adventure. The school is rebuilt—bigger, better, brighter than before. The boys may knock again on the mysterious portal of the past. What adventures wait then there? Will they hunt the king's deer with bold Robin Hood? Will they help Blondel to find the king? Will they avenge the grim fate of the Princes in the Tower? Behind the Shining Door the Winged Boy sits, his head resting on his hands, his wings folded on his shoulders. He is waiting for the sound of the knocker.